COURT OF DESTINY

An Urban Fantasy

ANN GIMPEL

CONTENTS

COURT OF DESTINY
MAGICK AND MISFITS SERIES, BOOK FOUR

An Urban Fantasy

By
Ann Gimpel

Tumble off reality's edge into a twisted world fueled by myth and magick

BOOK DESCRIPTION, COURT OF DESTINY

Urban fantasy and slow burn romance wrapped into a serial that will keep you up reading long into the night.

Strange bedfellows rock worlds.

Faery's castle lies in ruins, a reflection of the rest of a land I love. My land, my realm, has altered almost beyond recognition. The part that hasn't changed is the incredible people and creatures who live in Faery. Unicorns. Fauns. Satyrs. Fae. Sidhe. To name but a few. Their spirits have been indomitable, and it makes me proud to call them brothers.

But then, the Unseelie used to be brethren too. Now they stand against us along with a collection of monsters intent on sucking every last breath of life from Faery.

The worst part about all of this has been not knowing whom I can call friend. Faery, the incarnation of the land that bears her name, recovered her body, but I don't trust her. Our lead seer confessed her visions have been tainted. We are in the thick of things. As we lurch into the endgame, my life, soul, and fortunes are linked with the woman I love. We rise—or fall—together.

If it comes down to a gut-wrenching choice, will I pick Faery or Dariyah?

AUTHOR'S NOTE

Book covers play a big role in my creative process. I saw a set of covers featuring a badass Fae prince a while back and bid on them. Unfortunately, someone had a faster Internet connection than me, so I didn't end up with them. But everything comes out as it should because I found another cover I liked even better: the one on *Court of Rogues*, first of the Magick and Misfits books.

I've always been fascinated with the Otherworld. The faeries' ancestral home goes by many names. It's called *Annwn* in Welsh mythology and *Avalon* in Arthurian legend. In Irish mythology it's referred to as *Tír na nÓg, Mag Mell,* and *Emain Ablach*. Irish myths also feature a place called *Tech Duinn*, where the souls of the dead gather.

But I digress. My vision is a world where mortal and faery collide.

You, my readers, will let me know how well I managed it.

CHAPTER ONE, AURIL

Her travel spell took forever. It meant she'd waited nearly too long to return to the world where she'd lived for so many years. First with Dariyah, but then alone. The alone part had been both blessing and curse. She'd always treasured solitude, but the absence of anyone to talk with had worn on her.

"Eh, nothing is perfect," she murmured as the familiar flower scents of her previous home closed around her. She kicked open her magical well and sucked power like a starving child in a famine-ravaged country. Sinking into a crouch, she waited for a modicum of normalcy to return.

This world, this place, would never have sustained her and Dariyah if she hadn't married her magic with it. At first, the land had appeared suspicious because it steadfastly refused to communicate with her. Back then, she and her toddler had been on the run almost since she'd birthed the child.

She'd been tired and out of options. Or so she'd told herself. The tired part had been true, but surely there'd have been more alternatives if she'd gotten off her ass and looked for them. The kicker, though, had been her daughter gazing at her through the trusting eyes of the very young and begging to stay.

Auril understood why. Out of all the places they'd landed, this one was by far and away the most habitable. Not too warm, not too cold, with lush vegetation, rolling lands, and babbling brooks. So many spots they'd stopped had been freezing or boiling or barely had breathable air.

And so, she'd made this work, but there had been tradeoffs—serious ones. She had to have a method to replenish her power, and the only way it would happen here was if she loaned a good big bunch of herself to the land in return for tapping into its core.

Eventually, they'd developed a balance—all without exchanging a word. The cost had all been on her side. She'd forbidden the land to drain so much as an angstrom of magic from Dariyah. In the absence of any kind of compact, she'd assumed she'd have a battle on her hands one day. It never happened.

The world was content to draw from her and leave her daughter alone. Auril had a hunch it had to do with Pegasus's blood. Evil made most entities with pure magic nervous, and this world might fall into that category.

Her ragged breathing eased as power coursed through

her. She'd assumed once she returned to Faery, she'd trade what she'd received on this world for Faery's nourishment. It could still happen, but for now she'd made enough alterations in the fiber and weave of her magic, it no longer matched up with what she could glean from Faery.

Perhaps the spot Dariyah had labelled the *in-between* might work. It restocked her daughter's power, so it might work for her. If her stores hadn't been perilously low, she'd have tried it first. The only problem with that was she'd have to ask Dariyah where it was, which would reveal her problem. Everyone had enough on their plates. She wasn't keen on adding to Dariyah's worries. Not after a series of revelations that had shaken her daughter—and infuriated her too.

Auril set her mouth in a tight line. Decisions she'd made had taken a toll on everyone. She'd known a day would come when she'd have to come clean, but the admission about Dariyah's father was the toughest conversation she'd ever had. She couldn't have released the truth any sooner; it would have placed Dariyah at grave risk. What her daughter didn't know couldn't be wrested from her by force.

If Auril had her way, she'd never have loosed the truth, but events had caught up with her—just as she'd known they would. Seer ability could be a bitch; it shone light into twisted, unpleasant realities. Still refueling her power, she allowed herself the luxury of dipping her toes in the pity pool before snapping out of her sour mood.

After rising from a crouch, she made her way to a

cavern with an underground lake. It wasn't her favorite scrying location, but it was the strongest one by far. At least she wasn't swaying on her feet any longer. Neither was she teetering on the edge of falling on her face.

A humming vibrated in the pit of her stomach as she bent to enter the cave. Much like the cavern beneath Faery, this one was studded with crystals embedded in its rock walls. The floor was damp and sandy, and the gentle lapping of water indicated the lake was quiescent.

It could grow quite active when she was in the midst of a vision.

Auril clenched her teeth and paced in a circle. Visions. How could her prophecies have been so far off-base? She'd seen Dariyah fighting Pegasus in an aerial battle. It was why her daughter's wings had finally revealed themselves. To challenge her father to a lethal contest. Except it hadn't rolled out that way. Not even close.

Pegasus had captured Dariyah. While shackled by his power, she'd managed to free his prisoners, but if help hadn't arrived, she'd never have reunited her astral and physical selves. Eventually, she'd have faded to naught but spirit, stuck on a faraway world.

"Maybe I'm underestimating her." Auril continued to talk out loud.

Still, if she'd understood correctly, the only thing that saved Dariyah had been a dragon's quick thinking. Ash had liberated the tiny bit of her essence trapped within Pegasus's magical weave. Being reunited with her missing magic had allowed Dariyah to become whole again.

Pegasus was dead—or he should be. Set upon and eaten by the mages he'd imprisoned should have done the trick, but immortality could be tricky. The lead dragon, Ash, had carved out the horse's magical center, but even that could be reversed. It all depended how quickly Medusa and her Gorgon sisters had arrived at Pegasus's lair.

Auril closed her teeth over her lower lip. A far more relevant question was how many of the other events she'd seen had been bogus? And why? Was it a corollary of her long stint on this world? Had it warped her ability to birth true-seeing? The whys didn't matter, though. What did was how much of what she'd imparted to her compatriots back on Faery had been false?

They counted on her, based their strategy decisions on her information. If part of what she'd told them couldn't be relied upon, it was miraculous they'd won the last battle. In the future, she'd insist on corroboration from the dragons' seers before promulgating any of her visions as gospel.

And then, there was Danu, her goddess mother. Bitter words had fallen between them. Worse than bitter. Harsh. Angry. Unforgiveable. Auril hadn't sought out Danu for millennia, but neither had her mother reached out to her. As an exceptionally last resort—if it seemed the war was all but lost—she'd choke on humble pie and find Danu. She'd beg, grovel, even apologize, if it brought divine assistance to their sides.

It might not matter what she did. Danu could laugh in her face, spit invectives, and walk away. But at least Auril would have tried.

Wrenching her attention back to her scrying lake, she growled, "Talk to me," sending the words deep into the earth beneath her feet. Usually, she knelt near the lake, but she was too keyed up to sit in one spot. Auril wasn't expecting an answer. This world was stubborn and silent. Perhaps it was incapable of speech, but they could trade imagery. Hell, there were many paths they could have settled upon, but the stumbling block was this world. It wasn't interested in talking to her.

Time slithered past as she scribed a circle so many times she wore a path in the soft sandy dirt. Finally, she forced herself to walk toward her usual spot. Something about it drew her, except today the pull felt stronger than usual. Odd. Nothing about the cave—or this world—had changed.

Why was the combination of lake and sand almost crooning to her?

She stopped in her tracks, no easy task since her feet had developed a will of their own and kicked out as they did their damnedest to propel her body to the place she'd sat hundreds of times.

Perhaps thousands.

"I don't trust you," she said, inserting spaces between each word.

Her right foot quivered with the effort of holding it immobile. The energy swirling around her developed an even more compelling veneer. She'd never fought it before, but then it had never felt so...unnatural.

The flow of power, which had been robust, was drying

up. She slammed the gates of her reservoir just in case. Like any tank, its levels were a two-way affair. What flowed in could flow back out just as readily if the source decided she wasn't worthy.

Harsh laughter rolled from her as she hustled out of the cave. The magic endemic to this world was stronger in there than anywhere else. It was why she'd selected that spot for much of her scrying.

She sucked in a breath, blew it out, and did it a few more times to center herself. She'd lived here hundreds of years. Why had she never questioned the integrity of this world?

"Because it never gave me a reason to doubt it," she answered her own query. Beyond that, most worlds were neutral, benign. This one probably was too, except she'd misread its motives. She'd been convinced sharing her magic was what it wanted.

Sort of a mutually beneficial arrangement. She scratched its back, and in return it fueled her visions and kept her power up to snuff. Waves of invitation wafted from the cave. All she had to do was go back in, take up residence in her usual spot, and all would be well.

The land appreciated her, missed her, wanted every-thing to fall back into a pattern it had come to value, and—

"Stop!" Auril sliced a hand downward. "You lied to me, manipulated me. You and I are done."

You only believe we are. You are mine, skittered through her mind.

Auril fell back a pace before recovering herself. "I am

no one's but my own," she retorted hoping she'd struck a sufficiently assertive note.

Malevolent laughter rose all around her. Rocks cascaded from a nearby cliff. She executed a sideways leap to avoid being struck. Conversation wouldn't buy her anything, so she hurried to the cottage she'd constructed with a combination of her power and what she'd borrowed from the land.

Booms and crashes suggested the land had just withdrawn its contribution to her home. She broke into a run. She'd left things inside, scrolls and scrying implements she'd recover no matter how much rubble buried them.

"If I'm yours," she shouted, "you're treating me quite shabbily."

The land didn't answer. Big surprise since today's words were the first she'd heard in all the centuries she'd called this place home. The usual illusory curtain separating her cottage from plain view was still in place. She swept it aside with a thought and spit curses as the ruins of a dwelling she'd built with determination and sweat equity came into view.

One side had caved in, and the other was working on it thanks to earthquakes shaking it off its foundation stones. Auril didn't hesitate. If she gave away her position, the next part of the cottage to collapse would be right over her head. She hated to waste her newly resurrected magic, but she funneled some of it into a ward, hoping to buy herself a few minutes.

Everything she wanted to salvage was in one spot. For

once, her penchant for organization was paying off. Banking on stealth, she zigzagged, avoiding obstacles where she could and crawling over others. The cabinet holding her valuables was untouched. Wrapping the whole thing in a transport spell, she moved it out of harm's way, and herself along with it. All around her, the earth boomed and heaved; cracks extended outward in all directions, and the cottage dropped into a sinkhole.

Because she was working against the world, everything required an obscene amount of magic, but it couldn't be helped. She'd always prided herself on her ability to pivot with ever-changing circumstances, but she was rusty. The war provided challenges, but nothing like when she'd been on the run with her baby. Staying out of sight had been crucial. If anyone had found her, they'd have put two and two together, snatched Dariyah, and tried to do away with the mixed blood mage.

Auril would have fought to the death to keep it from happening. No matter who her adversaries turned out to be, the results wouldn't have been pretty. She hadn't had a leg to stand on, and she'd known it down to her bones. No moral high ground. Nope. That would have belonged to whomever carried out Faery's laws.

"Let it go," she instructed in sharp tones and riffled through the cabinet. If it wouldn't have been such a power hog, she'd have transported the whole thing to save time. A large sack would have been lovely, but she couldn't risk another trip into what had been her home. It sat well below ground level, and she'd run headlong into the world's fury if she risked a second trip.

After tucking items into pockets, she gathered the books and scrolls in her arms. While not as tapped out as when she'd traveled here, the return trip would drain her newly refreshed magic below acceptable levels.

Again.

She'd had to titrate her power all through the last battle. She didn't aim to be in that position a second time. Part of her depletion had occurred while pouring power into Dariyah after she'd returned from Pegasus's realm. Auril had done what she had to, not considering how difficult it would be for her to make up the difference.

Ripping and tearing alerted her it was time to go, before the jagged cracks, which were widening by the moment, reached the spot where she stood. Would the world stand in her way?

Almost certain the answer was yes, she dropped her warding in favor of tossing everything she had into a journey casting that encompassed her and her possessions. Not that she couldn't have made do without them, but they'd been trusty companions for too long to leave them here. Who knew who might stumble onto this place? She'd located it, which argued others could as well. Anyone who found her things could establish power over her.

The first tenet of magic is believing you can do what you've set out to. Auril visualized the Midnight Court, a place that was more hers than any other, and kindled her casting. Through the space of two long breaths, nothing happened. She was about to goose her casting, heedless of how much magic it took so long as it removed her from what had become a hostile situation.

Turned out, she didn't have to. Where she stood crumpled around her, traded for the familiar dimness of a teleport channel. Breath streamed from her in gasping pants. Her heart was pounding, and she recognized how unnerved she'd been by the specter of spending however long it would have taken for Dariyah to show up.

Her daughter would have figured things out eventually, but Auril hated to be the cause of wasted time, effort, and magic that would have been far better spent fighting to preserve Faery.

At least this visit had unearthed harsh truths, things she should have known—if she'd chosen to look. The only reason she'd been able to draw magic from the world was because of the détente they'd established. An agreement that was no more. Auril still didn't quite understand what she'd done to anger the world to such an extent. Had leaving done it? Or was it when she'd resisted the call to take up her usual scrying seat next to the lake?

Scrunching her tired eyes shut she reconstructed her visit. Everything had gone along fine until she'd questioned the accuracy of the visions she'd come up with. That was when everything turned to shit. For whatever reason, the world had been skewing her future-seeing.

She didn't believe the world held malevolent intent, or that someone like the Unseelie king was behind any of it. If he'd found her, he would have rousted her out and done his damnedest to end her. More likely, the world had been alone so long, its way of interacting was overlaying its two cents' worth into her scrying.

She rubbed her eyes before opening them. The motivations of her erstwhile home didn't make a difference. None at all. She had two priorities: figuring out how to add to her magic and letting everyone know her prophecies might have gaping holes in them. Two dragons had remained in Faery, but they weren't seers. She needed to consult with the dragons' blind seers once she'd solved the riddle of how to keep her magic flowing.

The Midnight Court recognized her. Of course, it did. She'd built the place from her essence and her blood. It had kept her from totally running aground magic-wise, but she needed a better solution. Damn. Her thoughts were racing in circles. That one had already popped up.

Titrating her magic to the smallest amount needed to keep her spell floating, she held the lore materials close. They were heavy, and her arms full, but she'd be back in Faery soon.

Soon turned out to be on the optimistic side. By the time her journey spell ceded to the glade surrounding the Midnight Court, she was panting with effort. Clearly, moving herself and her possessions hadn't been the swiftest decision, yet she hadn't had a choice.

Everything in her arms clunked onto the ground. She rocked from foot to foot, working on catching her breath and willing a tiny flow of magic from the Midnight Court to salvage her dilapidated energy.

"Sister. Whatever is the matter?" Titania strode to her side and bent to retrieve the lore books. "Ysir will want these for the library he's building."

Several inches shorter than her, Titania was staring speculatively out of golden eyes. With her white hair neatly braided and a fresh robe, she appeared somewhat rested.

"Are you going to tell me? Or not?" Titania pressed.

Complaining went against the grain; so did admitting she might have been wrong. Today was one for doing hard things, though. "It's possible some of my prophecies might not be accurate. We need to check them with the dragon seers' versions."

Drawing her white brows into a single line, Titania said, "And you came up with this how?"

"I returned to the world I spent all that time on."

"And? Come on, Auril, don't make me drag this out of you."

"The short answer is the land and I made a deal. It allowed me to tap magic from its core for Dariyah and me. In return, I shared power with it."

"And then you left." Titania nodded understanding.

Auril blew out a weary breath. She hadn't factored abandonment into the equation. "Aye," she agreed. "I left, and when I returned I harbored doubts about my scrying since Dariyah's battle with Pegasus was so far off the mark."

Titania offered a crooked smile. "Looks like you collected all your toys and left home."

"I did, indeed." Auril swayed on her feet. "I need mead and food and to sit a while. I barely made it back here."

"Faery will replenish your magic." Titania nodded briskly.

With such a strong a lead-in, Auril grabbed the bit between her teeth. "You see, there's my second critical problem, or probably my first since everything hinges on it."

"Keep talking," Titania urged.

Her sister's tone had softened, and it wasn't as wrenching as she'd feared to reveal the dilemma around her magic.

❧ 2 ☙

CHAPTER TWO, CYN

The gathering at the Midnight Court was bittersweet. We paid homage to those who'd fallen during the last battle. Originally, I'd planned to hash out what would happen next. I felt certain we wouldn't have much time between now and the next onslaught.

Even though I'd meant for this morning to be devoted to plans for proceeding, it never happened. First a faun, and then a phalanx of faeries, wanted to say a few words in remembrance for their friends who'd died, I didn't have it in me to stop them. Yes, we were at war, but some rituals took precedence over sketching out who'd fight next to whom. We needed to heal before we'd have the heart for more carnage.

I'd managed to make it through saying my own farewells as I lit the pyres sending the dead to their next life in the *Dreaming*. Ulane, one of the unicorns, and I had completed that sad task hours before. Maybe the little bit of down time I'd stolen with Dariyah at her empty apartment back on Earth had blunted my stoic side because a yearning for revenge rolled through me like a hot tide, annihilating everything in its wake.

If I had to personally dismember every single Unseelie, I'd do it. Nothing would bring my people back, but those who'd taken part in this ill-fated, poorly-thought-out war would pay. All of them. Once the Unseelie were out of the way, I'd start in on the Gorgons and Medusa's other son, Chrysaor. And the Shadow Lords.

All of a sudden, this war had taken on personal overtones. I recognized the danger, but I didn't care. My days of being Faery's regent in name only were over. I'd picked up the banner, and I'd run with it and make decisions that were best for my land and my people, no matter what the cost.

Tributes to the dead had run their course. Before I could steer us back to planning mode, Auril disclosed doubts about the accuracy of her future-seeing, and it hit me hard. Ysir too. Shock marched across his wizened features before he smoothed them to neutrality. He's been Faery's librarian forever, and he also dabbles in cartography and scrying.

"So," Auril went on, her deep musical voice strained, "I must confer with the dragon seers before we firm up our next set of battle plans."

"We're headed to Fire Mountain right after this,"

Dariyah told her mother. "You're welcome to share our travel spell."

Auril nodded briskly. "Thank you. I shall."

It seemed as if she wanted to say something further, but no more words came. Funny how things shake out the way they're meant to. Even if I'd tried to turn this meeting into a strategy session at its front end, Auril's problem would have overruled me.

Dariyah was gathering up debris from the breakfast we'd purchased at a Starbucks not far from her flat. Faery has no trash bins, so Dariyah dropped the bags and cups in a nearby firepit and doused them in magefire. Hustling back to where Auril and I stood, she said, "Ready. Do you know why Ash told us we needed to come?"

"Not exactly," I replied. "But my guess is they want to discuss something, and they didn't trust any type of communication beyond the borders of their world."

"That's exactly right," one of the two dragons who'd been assigned to remain in Faery rumbled. His (her?) red scales shimmered in the sunlight. His companion, a golden dragon, stood a few feet off to one side.

Last I'd seen them, Titania was showing them where a sheep herd was. "Did you get enough to eat?" I asked.

"Not really," the gold dragon said bluntly.

"Return and eat your fill," I said. "We need you at your maximum strength."

"We could eat them all." The red dragon puffed steam.

He might have been testing me. Titania hadn't been nearly as generous since she'd told them to only slake their hunger. "You probably could," I told him, adding, "Use your best judgment."

Before Titania, who was standing next to Ysir, lodged a protest about Faery having limited resources, I built a journey spell and draped it around Auril and Dariyah.

The Midnight Court dropped away. Dariyah slotted her power in with mine. When we were joined like this, I felt like one of the gods. As if I had enough magic to conquer worlds.

"What's wrong?" Dariyah asked her mother.

"What makes you think anything is?" Auril countered.

"Because I know you. Where'd you go? When we returned from Earth, you were gone."

I'm no expert at reading Auril's expressions. She was absent from Faery for centuries, but I thought something like chagrin creased her forehead. "I was going to tell you," she acknowledged, "but I was waiting until the right time. I went back to the place you grew up."

"Why?" Dariyah furled both russet brows.

She and her mother could have passed for twins with their long, unruly red hair and Valkyrie builds. Deeply chis-eled features suggested crossing either of them was a very bad idea. About the only difference between the two women was their eyes. Where Dariyah's were a clear, iridescent green, her mother's were silver. Dariyah's striking silver wings were another disparity. They'd only sprouted recently as the spell her mother had cast to keep them hidden crashed and burned.

"I returned to that world to replenish my magic." Auril stopped there.

"Can't you do that in Faery?" I asked, not understanding.

"If I could, I'd never have gone all that way." Auril locked gazes with me. "Something happened during the time I lived elsewhere. The weave of my power isn't a match for Faery any longer. I can suck small infusions from the Midnight Court, enough to keep me going, but at nowhere near my full strength."

"Odd," Dariyah murmured. "Since Faery is a decent complement for me."

"When we return, you can point me toward the place you used to go," Auril told her daughter.

"Of course. I stumbled onto it quite by accident and kept returning. I've never met anyone else there, but I've sensed traces of everything from shifters to Griffons."

Fascinating. An all-purpose well. "Wonder why I never heard about it," I murmured.

"Probably because you never had the need for such a thing," Dariyah replied crisply. "Necessity makes for odd bedfellows." Her nostrils flared. "We're almost there."

We were, indeed. This trip had gone quicker than I'd figured it would, even with our magic conjoined. "Any idea where the well that's all things to all mages taps power from?" I asked as my spell developed lighter edges.

Dariyah shook her head. "It's quite close to Earth. I always assumed someone—or a consortium of someones— had constructed it. Probably mages without a country, like

I was for so long." Glancing at her mother, she added, "You should have said something about your magic."

Auril shrugged. "I prefer to solve my own problems."

Dariyah snorted. "Stiff-necked."

"And you think you're not?" her mother retorted.

"We're not talking about me." Dariyah scrunched her features into a thoughtful expression. "Something must have happened on your world. Did the land cut you off or something?"

"Aye. Or something. Let's just say the cottage I built is no more, and neither of us will ever return there."

"Someday, I'd like to hear what happened," I tossed out.

"Someday, I may tell you," Auril said, "but right now, we have far more important items facing us than a distant pissed-off world."

My journey channel dissipated; the cracked dry plain that was a large part of Fire Mountain took shape around us. Faraway volcanoes belched smoke. Twin suns sat at the ten o'clock position radiating heat. Did they ever set? I had a feeling the answer was no, but I'd never spent enough time aboveground here to find out.

I scanned the skies for our usual greeting party, but it was empty of dragons—or anything else. The plain had sported groups practicing various maneuvers last time we'd been here, but it too sat empty.

"Where is everyone?" Dariyah turned in a full circle, a hand shading her eyes as she stared skyward. Her silver wings, courtesy of the winged steed who'd fathered her, were folded against her back.

"Don't know. Let's head for the caves. If the dragons aren't here, they must be there," I said and began walking in what I hoped was the proper direction. Fire Mountain is a strange world. A cluster of volcanoes belching smoke, fire, and lava circles the plain, but sometimes, the mountains form a line rather than a circle. Today was one of those times.

"A bit more to the left," Auril said.

Not questioning how she knew, I altered course.

Sweat oozed from every pore and dripped into my eyes. The heat was oppressive, but not as horrific as it had been before the dragons had linked their magic with mine and Dariyah's.

"At least this place keeps the riffraff down to bare minimums," Dariyah muttered.

"It's perfect for dragons," Auril said.

"My point exactly," Dariyah retorted. "Perfect for them, and not so great for the rest of us. Do you suppose those are the cliffs that lead to the caves?" She trained her gaze dead ahead.

"Hope so," I said. "They've been forming and vanishing by turns." The swoosh of wings drew my attention upward. "Finally," I muttered as Ash's golden bulk heaved into view.

In a startling departure from his usual elegance, he thudded to the ground a couple of meters away. "Get on," he bugled.

I waited until Auril was settled at the base of the dragon's neck and clambered up behind her. Dragon scales are sharp. And hot. But I wasn't about to complain.

"I'll fly," Dariyah announced.

"Figured as much," the dragon rumbled around smoke and ash as he shot skyward.

Dariyah flew slightly behind and off to one side. Flight had come easily to her, even though she'd harbored doubts about the wings being clumsy. I took a long moment to savor the graceful way they cut through the hot, still air before asking, "Where is everyone? Is something unusual in the works?"

Ash didn't answer me. Much like Faery is a personification of the land that bears her name, Ash plays a similar role for the dragons and Fire Mountain. He is both dragon lord and an elemental part of this world. We flew through a break between two mountains and headed toward an unexpected grove of odd-looking trees with smooth orange bark and medallion-shaped green leaves.

I hadn't known anything grew here.

Startled by the noise of our approach, a herd of wildebeests made a break for it, running flat out across the plain. Except it wasn't as arid on this side. The occasional bush grew along with scraggly clumps of prairie grass. After clearing the trees, Ash circled for a landing next to a large, still lake.

Today was one for surprises. I'd thought the only water on this world was deep in the dragons' cave system. Several dragons stood near the lake. Others were half-hidden in the trees. The air smelled steamy, not unlike a tropical jungle.

We were on the ground, and I jumped down, fashioning

a cushion of magic to break my fall. Auril was already on the move. Presumably, she'd spotted Goren and Brynn, the blind dragon seers. Dariyah touched down, furled her wings, and walked toward me.

"Who would have thought?" she murmured as she glanced at the water and vegetation.

I nodded, waiting to see why we were here and not in the caves.

"You took longer getting here than I'd imagined you would, but your late arrival was fortunate," Ash began. "Had you arrived when I expected, you'd have run into the middle of our skirmish with the Shadow Lords." He shrugged amid the rattle of scales. "Seems they got the feel of our magic last time we imprisoned them. This time, they made short work of my spell. I suspect they had help from the Gorgons, which brings me to my second bit of bad news."

"Let me guess," Dariyah cut in dryly. "Daddy dearest didn't die after all."

"You shouldn't joke about such things," Ash rebuked her. "It would have been better had I not excised his magical center. His mother chivvied him back to life, but he's gone totally mad. Before, he was picky about who he killed, but now he's rampaging through cities on Earth killing everything in his path."

"I thought his prisoners turned him into dinner," I muttered. I'd seen them carving chunks off him. Why hadn't that been the end of it?

"His altered appearance might be a contributing factor

to his mental distress," Ash said. "The Gorgons used snakes to patch up the holes and missing spots, and now he's as ugly on the outside as he is within."

"Yuck. Now there's an unappetizing visual." Dariyah made a sour face.

"Why doesn't Medusa do something about his killing spree?" I asked. One of the tenets all mages at least pay lip service to is not interfering with mortals. The Unseelies' inability to comply had signed their death knell in Faery and was why they'd been banished.

"She doesn't care," Ash said. "She's always been a wee bit on the crazy side herself, but she generally hid away on that island of hers with the other Gorgons and didn't bother anyone."

I'd been listening to the exchange. Ash had told us about Pegasus's untimely revival for a reason. "Are you expecting us to drop everything and go after him?"

"Someone has to," Ash said. "Dragons don't mingle in mortal affairs, but this predicament is my doing." He shook himself from head to toe and blew a stream of smoke off to one side. "I don't possess an alternate form. If I showed up on Earth, I'd create more problems than I solved."

"You had no choice," Dariyah protested. "I'd have faded away if you hadn't acted."

"True, but that part isn't important," Ash told her. "I should have done a more thorough job ending him."

Dariyah exhaled long and slow. "The critical part is intervening before he destroys more than he already has."

"Precisely," the dragon said.

"Why are we here and not in the caves?" I asked.

"We're still cleaning them up," Ash replied. "It's where the Shadow Lords chose to materialize."

"What happened to them?" Dariyah asked.

Good question. I wanted to know too.

The dragon's jaws parted in a tooth-filled grin. "Dungeons. I try not to repeat my mistakes. I didn't believe the vortex I wrapped the Shadow Lords in back on Faery would hold them for long, but I had no idea they'd break free quite so quickly. I assumed I had at least a hundred years before they clawed their way through."

"What's different about the dungeons?" I looked up at the dragon, meeting his whirling gaze with difficulty.

"They are fiery pits, surrounded by rivers of lava. No one has ever escaped. They won't either."

"Why didn't you put them there in the first place?" Dariyah folded her arms under her breasts.

"We did not wish such evil to be that close. We've gotten past that."

"Did you imprison all of them?" After wincing at Dariyah's candor, I asked the second critical question.

"Nay. Six. Once they were squealing like a pack of wild pigs, the rest hightailed it away from Fire Mountain before we could corral them."

"Is that half of them?" I was still feeling my way forward.

"It's our best guess," Ash concurred.

"Six is better than twelve," I muttered.

"Aye, but they will be clamoring for revenge. Back to

Pegasus," Ash said. "Not so long ago, you said you were in my debt. I'm calling it due and requesting your aid."

I nodded solemnly. Such was his right. I could refuse, but what would that make me? A man with no honor. "I will do everything I can to find the horse and defeat him once and for all," I said, "but I need you and the dragons to do something while I'm occupied."

"And that might be?" Ash raised a scaled brow.

"Figure out how to blow up the Unseelie's staging area. The world where Oberon held Titania prisoner. It's been the next task on my list for a while now."

"Done," Ash said.

"You're not going after Pegasus alone," Dariyah declared.

Words rose about it being too dangerous, but I held them in the safety of my throat. Even if I told her to remain behind, she wouldn't, and it would turn into a bone of contention between us.

Auril and the two dragon seers were walking our way. "Thank you," she told Brynn and Goren.

"Anytime," one of the seers replied. Probably Brynn since his wings were a wee bit lighter.

Auril clasped her hands together and announced. "I am coming to Earth with you."

"How's your magic?" I asked in as close to a neutral tone as possible. That type of query is unspeakably rude among my people, but if she needed to travel to Dariyah's refueling spot, it could set us back by a couple of hours.

"Fine. Turns out Fire Mountain was more than willing to replenish my stores."

"What happens once we get to Earth?" Dariyah asked without preamble, eyeing her mother closely.

I girded myself for the usual barrage of double meanings and ambiguous statements typical of seers.

"We should win," Auril said.

"Should?" I cocked my head to one side.

She made a slight shrugging motion. "These things are never cast in stone. The quicker we get moving, the better our odds. Pegasus's magical center is damaged. He cannot hold onto power, which means he must constantly restock himself. Hence, the ongoing bloodbath."

"How does that work?" Dariyah asked. "Killing someone never strengthened me."

"You never drank your victim's blood," Goren bugled.

"All blood holds a modicum of power," Brynn added.

"Too bad it doesn't last long," the other seer said.

"What about the rest of your future-seeing?" I asked Auril.

"Eh. Not as warped as I'd feared. In some spots I was missing critical elements. In others, I'd come to conclusions that weren't warranted."

I waited, but she didn't elucidate. She hadn't spent all that long with the seers, but perhaps they had their own ways of dealing with her type of problem. Various kinds of magics overlap considerably, but it doesn't hold true for seers. They're in a class by themselves.

"We should probably include a few others," I said and

considered who we could conscript to help take Pegasus down. So many of Faery's creatures can't construct a glamour that covers hoofs or wings or eyes no human would ever possess.

"Do not overfill your ranks," Brynn cautioned.

"Aye, what we have seen suggests stealth will win out over brute force," Goren murmured.

"We will work on the problem of the Unseelie's world," Ash reassured me.

I bowed formally. "Thank you. We shall return once our task is complete."

Casting a journey spell, I moved us away from Fire Mountain. My promise to report in once we'd presumably done away with Pegasus was wildly optimistic. Not the checking in part, but the killing segment. If the tableau that had unfolded in his lair hadn't been enough to do the trick, I wasn't certain anything would.

"The crux," Auril said, "will be keeping him separate from Medusa and her sisters until he has moved beyond where anyone can salvage what's left of him."

She'd obviously been helping herself to my thoughts, but I was getting used to it. Besides, it was a minor point balanced against the task ahead. "Do you have ideas about how to finesse that?" I asked.

Auril offered a grim smile that underscored the otherworldly portion of her appearance. No one looking at her now would ever mistake her for mortal. "The dungeons in the bowels of Fire Mountain might fit the bill. I have the coordinates, and we should be able to ferry him there and get out before the fires damage us."

Great. Peachy. Now all we had to do was locate him, immobilize him somehow, and teleport him to Fire Mountain, hoping against hope he didn't wake up mid transport.

Dariyah grasped my hand and squeezed hard. "We'll make it work," she said.

"Not a thought to call my own, eh?" I teased.

"Never again," both women said almost in unison.

Something about the absurdity of the situation struck me as funny. I was still laughing when my travel spell imploded leaving us standing ankle-deep in the lush grass of the Midnight Court.

Auril ran lightly across the glade, presumably to alert Titania. I turned Dariyah to face me and threaded my arms around her shoulders. "Are you good with this?"

"Why wouldn't I be?"

"He's your father."

She brayed laughter. "Yeah. One I never knew about until a few days ago. Besides, it takes more than stray sperm to make a dad. I want him dead probably more than you do. I'm who he kidnapped and planned to kill."

I hadn't forgotten, but family ties are funny things, and I'd had to ask the question. I drew her against me and tucked her head into the hollow between my neck and shoulder. We'd go in, strike quick, and be done with it. I hated to take time—and magic—away from the Unseelie war, but it was necessary.

After sifting through potential companions, I put out a

call in shielded telepathy to Ysir and Helmet, the Sidhe who maintained our arsenal. Too bad unicorns would stick out like sore thumbs. While not as in-your-face-impossible as a dragon would be, anything like a unicorn or a satyr or a faun or nymph would make it much harder to keep this task flying beneath the radar.

We'd be six. It would have to be enough. Presumably, humans had already launched a campaign to rid themselves of Pegasus. Maybe we could piggyback onto it, without revealing who we were.

The more I thought about it, the better I liked the idea.

CHAPTER THREE, DARIYAH

It didn't take long before we were assembled and ready to go. A final check of everyone's glamour necessitated a few last minute adjustments. I wasn't used to covering up my wings, and pointed ears have a way of poking through. If a mortal did catch a glimpse—of ears, not wings—they'd probably shrug it off and assume we were cosplaying scenes from *Lord of the Rings*.

The only member of our contingent I hadn't met before was Helmet. Medium height and burly, with a Slavic cant to his features, he appeared dependable. Where most Fae are on the slender side, his barrel-chested build was garbed in leather. A scabbard holding a wicked-looking blade was strapped across his back. Coal-black hair was braided close to his head, and his eyes were a gunmetal shade.

"We'll start out at Lady Luck," Cyn said. "It's a spot I can dial up news on a computer, and we can make decisions from there."

"Is that the place you staked out for yourself on Earth?" Helmet asked in a deep, gravelly voice.

"Aye," Cyn replied and narrowed his eyes. "The only one of you who's been there is Dariyah."

"I've seen it in visions," Mother spoke up.

I glanced her way. "You've been spying on me?"

Her generous mouth twitched at the corners. "Would you expect less of me?"

I elbowed her and called it even. The comfortable feel of Cyn's magic with its whiskey-and-wildflower scents wrapped around me; I inhaled hungrily. Being in love was new for me, very new. So new I fought to wrap my mind around it. Because of my mixed magics, I've never fit anywhere. On Earth, I had to pass for human. Up until very recently, my hybrid parentage was a death sentence in Faery. The cornerstone of even something as simple as friendship, let alone a love relationship, is honesty.

Since I couldn't be forthright, I'd kept to myself. What was the point of a house built on lies?

Cyn and I were mates, partners. He'd been drawn into the fiasco with my father because of me. Being diverted from the war that was ripping his land to bloody shreds was killing him, but because he was Cynwrigg ap Llyr, he'd do the right thing.

Or maybe it was because he loved me with a fierceness

equaling my own. I started to apologize, but didn't. He'd have shushed me, reminded me Ash had his talons in this particular circus. And then he'd grin in an engaging way that made him look about twenty and tell me everything wasn't about me.

Except in this instance, it was. If I hadn't come into his life, none of these dominoes would have clattered into place. I wouldn't have found Mother, wouldn't know about the war in Faery, and the secret of who'd fathered me would have remained shrouded in mystery.

"Two can play that game," Cyn spoke into my mind. He'd transported us to the stairs beneath the casino, and we'd begun traipsing up them.

"What game?" May as well feign innocence until I knew what he was getting at.

"Do you truly wish we'd never met?" The question was serious, but his eyes sparkled with warmth in the dim light of the stairwell. He knew the answer but was playing devil's advocate.

"Of course not, silly."

He laced his fingers with mine. *"Then don't waste energy on what-ifs. We're here. We'll do what we can to stop Pegasus. The Unseelie aren't going anywhere. Maybe the dragons will hit a jackpot and do away with their world. Even if they only cripple it, their efforts will reduce the odds of more Unseelie joining the war."*

"Maybe it will cut the heart out of them and they'll take their ball and go home." I'd switched back to talking out loud, but softly.

A long low whistle probably came from Ysir. "How big is this place, Regent?"

We'd been leading the way up the stairs. Cyn turned and held up a hand. "My Earth name is Jedediah Rolfson. Call me Jed here."

"Why?" Ysir's tone reflected shock.

"I needed a name that would blend in, not one that would always raise eyebrows."

"Understood, Regent, er Jed." Ysir snapped off an approximation of a salute.

"How about if I teleport everyone to your office?" I suggested. "That way you can do your usual walk-through on the way up."

"I was about to suggest the same." He squeezed my hand before letting go, and I whisked everyone to his office on the casino's top floor. Because he kept it locked, I wasn't expecting to shave ten years off anyone's life. As I'd wagered, the smallish room sat empty.

Titania placed her hands on her hips and turned in a circle. Pursing her lips into a disapproving expression, she said, "He can't do better than this?"

I made an effort to view his office through her eyes. It was on the spartan side with linoleum flooring, a large scarred oak desk, a rather shabby leather couch, and a card table with two chairs.

"He's not a prince here," I reminded Faery's queen. "Or even a regent. He's just another fellow running a casino."

"But surely..." she began before apparently deciding she was beating a dead horse.

"Make yourselves comfortable," I suggested and walked around the desk. I didn't have Cyn's password to get into his computer, but telepathy was stellar for things like that. Soon his machine hummed to life, and I shuffled through news stations, reading as I went.

Mother hung over one of my shoulders. "So that's a computer. I've seen them in my visions. What exactly can they do?"

"Almost everything except magic."

"Are all those things true?" Mother tapped the screen with her index finger.

Breath rattled from me. "True is relative when it comes to mortals and their news channels. Some are more reliable than others, but it appears Father has struck many places."

"Fear and chaos," Mother muttered. "They're his specialty. Must be empowering to finally be out in the open. Before, he hid behind a glamour to wreak havoc, and he always stopped after a rape and murder—or two."

Ysir, Helmet, and Titania were also ranged behind me. Apparently, the siren call of modern electronics had been too much to resist. A staunch knock on the door snapped my head up.

"Is anyone in there?" a man's voice called. He sounded nervous. Made sense. Cyn hadn't been here in a few days, and the distinct sounds of conversation wafting from his supposedly locked and sealed office would give any employee wandering the halls pause.

"Thanks for checking, Miles," Cyn boomed and

unlocked the door. Normally, he'd have dispensed with his key, but not when a mortal was standing by watching.

Miles stared at us, and we stared back. Like all casino employees, he was garbed in black slacks and a white shirt with the Lady Luck logo—a phoenix sinking into a crater —emblazoned on its pocket. "Are we, uh, hosting a costume party, boss?"

I wanted to snicker, but didn't. Out of all of us, Cyn and I were the only ones dressed in Earth-style clothing.

"Considering it." Cyn offered a sunny smile. "These good folks, or the three standing, are from Northwest Costume and Saddlery. They're trying to sell me a package for fall."

"I see." Miles nodded. A thick hank of reddish hair fell across one eye; he swept it out of the way. "Good to see you back, boss. Will you, erm, be here for a while?"

"Not this time, I'm afraid, but next week my calendar is much clearer."

"Good. Good. Things go better when you're here." Miles bobbed his head again. Most mortals are nondescript, but he could have been the poster boy for unexceptional. Seemingly having a hard time taking his eyes off the crew behind me, he backed out of the room and pulled the door shut behind him.

"I swear, Cyn—" Titania began.

Before she could launch into rebuking him for falling so far beneath his station, he chopped a hand downward. "Not now, and the name is Jed." Addressing his next words to me, he said, "What'd you find?"

I locked the door with a shot of magic and draped a sound shield around the room. No reason to make Cyn appear any odder than his staff already thought he was.

"The condensed version is Pegasus started in Europe, hitting some of the big cities. Seems fifty is his magic number. Once they're dead, he moves to his next target. He crossed to New York two days ago. So far, he's hit it, Boston, and Philadelphia. I figured he'd stay on the East Coast, but the most recent reports place him in Chicago."

I'd continued to read as I talked. "Oops, looks like fifty isn't cutting it. He mowed through 200 in Chicago."

"Why are humans not doing anything?" Titania demanded. "Do they usually sit on their duffs and wait to be rescued?"

It was a fair question. "Special forces and local police in Europe tried to bring him down. Nothing they've hit him with has had any effect. Once he showed up here, the National Guard was deployed."

"Their military hardware would be useless since he's immortal," Cyn muttered. "Maybe he's even more bullet-proof than before since his most vulnerable place is his magical center, and it's been altered."

I wrested my gaze from the screen and gave him my full attention. "So, how are we going to manage what modern weaponry hasn't been able to?"

"Child." Mother lapsed back into her pet name for me, and it grated. "How can you begin to compare magic to anything mortals wield?"

I wasn't about to launch into a description of contemporary ordnance. Granted the horse could repair most any wounding, but eventually his resources would thin out. Speaking of which, I noted, "He's needing to kill more, which suggests he's running into problems keeping himself together."

"Good point," Helmet agreed. "We should strike now, before he figures out a method to revive his flagging magic."

"The problem is where to locate him," Cyn said.

"He was in Chicago a few hours ago," I replied.

"Doesn't mean he remained there once he drained the corpses." Cyn voiced the obvious.

Mother sighed. I recognized that sigh. It meant she'd come up with a potential solution, but none of us would like it. "We have to let him know we're here," she said. "Then we can lure him to us." She placed a hand on my shoulder. "It pains me to do this, but you're the best bait we have. He'll blame you for his current predicament, and I bet he'll be stupid enough to come running if you call him out."

I swiveled to face her. "I have a better idea. Rather than challenging him to a duel at dawn, I can tell him I've had second thoughts. After all, he is my father. Yada. Yada."

Mother scrunched her forehead into a welter of lines. "He's arrogant enough, it just might work. In his book, he's the most important player, and he's always up for adulation, no matter which quarter it comes from." Her frown deepened. "In your case, it could do double duty. He'd be drawn because he yearns to have you worship him, but it would also offer proximity."

"So he can finish what he began," I said dryly.

"I'm opposed to using Dariyah as a lure. Period," Cyn growled.

"Hiding ourselves might pose a problem," Titania murmured, totally ignoring Cyn's protest, "but not one we can't move beyond."

"You weren't listening." Cyn's tone could have carved cracks in granite.

"I was"—Titania drew herself up tall, which placed the top of her head a bit above the center of Cyn's chest—"but Dariyah is our best option. We'd be fools to twist ourselves into pretzels launching a far more complicated plan with less chance of success."

"I don't like it," Cyn persisted.

"Get over it," Titania snapped. "I don't 'like' a lot of things. But being gone from Faery right now carries its own set of risks."

I snapped my fingers to cut the flow of what was turning into an argument, and not the type where anyone had a glimmer of winning. "Got it," I said brightly. "I'll slather on the sugar and ask if he could pretty please meet me in Carlsbad Caverns. If we kill the electricity, I mean really kill it so it takes humans days to effect a fix, that would be perfect. There are hundreds of rooms down there, caves and side caves and sub caves off of them. It would offer everyone ideal spots to hide because all that rock will redirect our magical emanations."

"He'll know someone is there, but not who or where." Mother's frown shifted to a determined expression.

"I like the cave part," Cyn said. "We can conscript the bats to aid us. They'll be messengers from cavern to cavern, so we won't need to employ telepathy. But I'm still not sold on hanging Dariyah out like a worm on a hook."

I'd forgotten about the bats. Carlsbad was home to hundreds of them. Maybe thousands. I pushed to my feet. We had a plan. No reason not to launch it. Another knock sounded at the door. I dismantled my privacy shielding. Cyn unlocked the door and pulled it open.

Kitchen staff rolled carts into the already-crowded office.

"What's all this?" Titania asked.

"Food," I told her.

She cast a long-suffering look my way. "Nothing wrong with my nose, dearie. Perhaps I should have asked why eating is more important than getting moving."

Cyn thanked his employees and hustled them back out the door. "We need to be at the top of our game," he said, "which means we're well-fed. Dig in, everyone."

"I'd have preferred a choice," Titania mumbled under her breath as she grabbed a covered dish off one of the carts. I might have been the only one who heard her, and I let it go. Being a queen couldn't be easy, particularly one who'd spent half a century in exile. Maybe by the time we were done with everything, she discard her "royalty is special" mindset.

I hoped so. Mother had managed to throw off the yoke

of liegedom. If she could do it, so could Titania. I dug into a ham sandwich and a bag of potato chips. Lunch food, so maybe it was midday here. I'd been too busy to look out Cyn's dirty window.

I purposefully wasn't thinking about coming face to face with the winged horse again. Even before whatever crazed mindset he'd slid into, he'd been one cold bastard. What I wanted to do was teleport the fuck out of here to my apartment and wrap my arms around my cat. I buried that thought deep, spading heaps of magic over it. I faced my problems squarely, muscled them aside, and kept on trucking. Or I used to.

What had changed? My magic was stronger than ever, so that couldn't be it. Probably, I'd had one too many close calls. The constant fighting was wearing on me. Other than a few stolen moments with Cynwrigg, I'd either been waging war or preparing to fight or struggling to escape for months.

Are we planning to throw a pity party? One of my less kind inner voices inquired archly.

Usually, I'd have snarked back, answering myself. Today, the concept of anything as prosaic as a pity party amused me. I'd thought Oberon stalking me had been bad. I'd had no clue it was the beginning of a long slide down a slippery slope into a goddess-damned shithole.

I'd been eating mindlessly. When my fingers grazed the ceramic plate, I glanced down and realized I'd polished off everything. No further reason to tarry, which meant it was showtime. I could get the luring part underway, but I couldn't do it from here. Telepathy is a two-way street, and it could lead Pegasus right to us.

Lady Luck held too many hapless humans who'd turn into collateral damage.

"I'm going to kick this can down the road. The sooner we get on with things, the sooner we'll be able to return to Faery," I said as I stood.

Cyn was on his feet and by my side so fast his movements were a blur. "I'll be right next to you."

"Not a good idea. Pegasus is shrewd enough to check if I'm alone, and your magical signature pulses like a beacon."

Cyn gripped my upper arm. "You are not going alone."

"She has to," Mother spoke up, followed by, "Maybe not."

"What are you thinking?" Titania asked her sister.

"I'll be in the Carlsbad vicinity," I informed everyone. Not willing to wait around while a debate ensured, I began cobbling a travel spell together.

"With me," Mother said firmly. After pushing upright, she walked to my other side. "Sorry, Cynwrigg, but my power is close enough to Dariyah's it might not kick off Pegasus's suspicions he's being played."

"Do not leave her side." Cyn punctuated his words by stabbing the space between mother and him with an index finger.

"I love her too," Mother reminded him.

I rolled my eyes. "Stand down. Both of you. I got along fine for centuries on my own—without either of you."

"So? You are not doing this by yourself," Mother repeated Cyn's sentiments.

"You're welcome to come with me," I told her.

"I wasn't aware I needed your permission." Her silver gaze bored into me.

Recognizing we were about to go rounds, I shut up. Nothing I could say would change her control freak tactics.

"We'll meet you in the caverns," Cyn said. He still didn't sound particularly happy, but he understood the need for expediency.

"Aye, and we'll take care of the electricity problem," Helmet said. In the short time I'd spent with him, he'd impressed me as quietly competent, not a man who wasted words. If he said he'd chop the flow of power, I believed him.

"I have a few ideas how we can finesse that." Cyn launched into outlining them.

His words faded as I snatched Mother in my journey casting and set a course for the Guadalupe Mountains in the southeastern corner of New Mexico. "Did you see this part?" I asked. "When you were comparing notes with the dragon seers."

"Not exactly."

I waited, but naturally Mother didn't add anything to her cryptic comment. I didn't waste breath feeding her more questions. Instead, I filled her in on how I planned to move forward.

"I'll bring us out a little way from the caverns. They're a national park, and a popular one, so there will be a lot of tourists and park staff. The caves are something like 800 feet underground and dependent on elevators to shuttle visitors around. There are stairs and ramps, but absent power, things will be chaotic until they manage to clear everyone out of there."

"Have you made a habit of mingling with mortals?"

Mother's question took me by surprise. "Um, yeah. Who else would I have been with? Faery was barred to me."

"Perhaps I'll spend some time here once we get past the problems plaguing Faery. My last forays to Earth were a very long time ago."

"No planes or cars, huh?"

"Um-hum. Try sailing ships. And precious few of them. People lived out their lives in the same spot they were born, for the most part."

"Believe it or not, I remember those times too. You'd find contemporary Earth interesting, and I have a place you can stay. Hang on. We're nearly at Carlsbad." To be on the safe side, I draped a ward around us. The high desert typical of the Southwest stuttered into view. Sagebrush, Joshua trees, and washes where water had carved runnels into the earth on the rare occasions rain showed up.

"Nicely done." Mother shaded he eyes with a hand and turned in a circle.

"Sometimes a blind dog finds a bone," I murmured pleased we'd landed roughly where I'd expected. Nothing around us but wilderness. No homes. No people.

"Where are these caverns?" Mother asked.

"That way." I pointed. "Maybe a mile away. We should get closer so we can keep an eye on how things are going with the others cutting the power." I'd thought things through and decided not to give my luring pitch the full court press until we were established in the caverns. That wouldn't happen until the lights had been doused.

"How will we know?"

I laughed. "Oh, we'll know. Humans are uber dependent on electricity. Alarms will blare, and you'll see a whole lot of activity."

Mother smiled, a rare enough occurrence I looked twice. Her usually harsh expression softened, and her beauty shone through. I snapped my glamour into place and began walking, threading my way around desert plants. Because it was easier going, I picked a gorge and followed it.

The next time I looked at Mother, she'd swathed herself in magic that gave her dark hair, twenty-first century trousers, running shoes, and a blue T-shirt blazoned with *Magic Rocks, Live the Dream.*

"That's a hoot. Where'd you come up with it?" I asked.

Mother shrugged. "Who knows where these things come from. Will I blend in if we're spotted?"

"Yup."

We covered the remaining distance in a companionable silence and ended up on a knoll overlooking the complex. All the parking lots were quite full. I'd lost track of days, but this must be a weekend judging from the crowds.

Because we had time, I pulled out my phone and looked for news.

"Handy little device," Mother said.

"It can be," I murmured as I scrolled. "Oooh, look at this." I angled the display so she could see too.

"Salt Lake City? Where is that?"

"Not all that far from here. Wonder why he's moving west?" I kept reading, and a partial answer formed. One of the military special force units had hit Pegasus with darts seeded with radioactive material.

Mother's fingers dug into my arm as she read over my shoulder. "I don't need anything fancy. Tell me what that means."

I dropped my phone into a pocket. "They tried to shoot him out of the sky. When it didn't work, they shot him with darts that hold a substance that should eat him up from within."

"Will it work?"

"Who knows? If he were mortal, sure. But then if he were mortal, all the other shit they did would have done the trick. For all I know, polonium-210 will strengthen him, but what it should do is dissolve his body, and damned fast."

"Pegasus incorporated the Gorgons' vipers," Mother reminded me.

"Eh. Way too many variables and unknowns."

Distant shouts and the blare of an alarm told me Cyn and Helmet had done their part. "Time to go?" Mother arched a red brow.

Rather than answer, I moved us underground aiming for the largest of the caverns. We'd set up shop there and hope I was sufficient bait to nab the winged horse's attention. If the radioactive isotope had burned him too badly, he might put his tail between his rear legs and hightail it back to his mother's island.

We'd find out soon enough.

CHAPTER FOUR, CYN

We sent joined magic down the main power trunks, instructing it to melt every junction box along the way. Because the lines were already in place, and all the magic had to do was follow them, it didn't require much effort at all. Once we ignited our spell, we teleported a short distance away to make certain we'd succeeded. Helmet had a decent working knowledge of electricity, which astonished me because it meant he'd spent time on Earth. It's rare for Faery's residents to leave, and Earth is far from a preferred destination ever since humans stopped believing in magic.

I figured the park service had to have emergency generator backup, so I wasn't surprised when the roar of gasoline-powered engines filled my ears. Along with a loud, annoying siren.

The generators would give the park enough juice to

hustle everyone out of the caves while they went to work addressing the problem. The town of Carlsbad wasn't far, but it wasn't much of a town, either. The nearest city was probably Las Cruces. Workmen would launch from there to fix the damage we'd created. It meant we had several hours—maybe as much as a few days—to deal with Pegasus.

If he even showed up. I'd checked the news, and the National Guard had done their damnedest to shoot him full of a very lethal radioactive isotope. One that would kill a mortal within hours. For all I knew, it would turn the horse into some kind of lethal super stud, spewing radioactive waste in his wake.

"I believe we're done here." Ysir tapped my shoulder.

We were. Time for step two. I'd visited Carlsbad Caverns, but it had been several years ago. The best place to start would be the cave frequented by bats to see if they'd be willing to help us. Taking care we were well shrouded, I led the way to the rear entrance. It had been designed to move material too large for the elevators in and out of the caves and for people who wanted to walk rather than ride the elevator down.

The bats flew this way and that like crazed rats with wings. "It's the alarm," I said. "It hurts their ears, and kills their echolocation ability because they can't hear their own sounds."

"I can fix that," Titania said and built a hasty tent around several groups of bats. Perhaps a hundred in all, they flocked to Faery's queen, perching on every available bit of her. Those who missed out on a spot of prime real estate fluttered to her feet.

I'd had no idea she possessed such an affinity for animals.

Cooing and whistling, she explained the bad noise would end soon and asked if they'd aid our cause. Watching her with them made me smile and long for Faery when my land hadn't been at war. Despite her high-handed, sometimes annoying ways, Titania represented the best of Faery as she communed with the bats.

She didn't have to request their assistance. She'd rescued them from the noise from hell, and they'd have laid down their furry little lives for her if she'd asked. When she was done talking, several bats flew to us, taking up posts on everyone's shoulders. We ended up with two bats apiece.

"Thank you little brothers," I said.

"Sissstersss," my pair corrected me.

"Many apologies."

They chittered and squeaked in response. Meanwhile, a steady stream of people walked around Titania's domed enclosure. They couldn't see it, but they sensed something was in their path and avoided it handily. Most of the visitors would exit via the elevators, but a hardy few walked up the long ramp from the bottom.

At least the infernal siren was finally silent.

Worry about Dariyah gnawed at me, but calling to her might compromise her position. I'd wait until I was close enough to hustle to her side in case something went wrong.

Titania dismantled her casting, and we marched forward. Still invisible behind wards, we passed a thinning bunch of mortals on their way to their cars.

By the time we descended to the cavern's upper levels, we were alone. Emergency lighting was dimming, so I kindled a mage light. The bat on that side shrieked unhappily, so I repositioned the illumination to stream from behind me and dialed it back to bare minimums.

A red light flashed off to one side. "Oops," I told the others. "No mage lights. Not until they turn off the generators. They have cameras down here, and they're scanning to make certain no one got left behind. Could turn into a big fat lawsuit for them."

"What's that?" Ysir asked.

"Something humans who think they've been wronged do to try to get rich quick," Helmet said, adding, "They're ridiculous."

I chuckled softly. "Someday, you'll have to tell me about your time on Earth."

"Someday, I will, Regent."

I deployed threads of enchantment, hunting for Dariyah and not finding her. "Can you locate your sister?" I asked Titania.

"Nay, and I've been looking."

Worry stabbed me dead in the guts. I was linked to Dariyah; Titania and Auril shared blood. For that fact, so did Titania and Dariyah. Why couldn't we sense them? Seeking spells had far greater range than what I was asking mine to do. I tried again with the same lack of results and picked up my pace.

We'd been gradually edging downward until the path leveled off, and I figured we'd hit the bottom of the primary tourist area. More caves below us were accessible via a network of ladders. People who are into caving often sign up for guided spelunking tours, but I've never seen the allure. Earth isn't sentient like Faery, but surely she resents mortals tunneling into her innards.

The muted hum of the generators shut off abruptly. I fired my mage light again, mindful of my bat companions. "We're looking for two women who are our friends," I told them. "Could you help us find them?"

The bats took off with a flurry of wings, the high-pitched squeals of their navigation gradually fading.

"Good idea," Titania said and added some clucking and cooing. The rest of the bats followed the first two.

"Should we wait for them?" Ysir asked.

"Nope. We keep walking," I replied. Taking a chance, I raised my mind voice to call Dariyah in shielded telepathy. I hadn't expected her to answer, and she didn't. Something about the mixture of rock and water and twisting, turning tunnels was even more effective shielding us from one another than I'd expected it to be.

"We should have picked a meeting spot," Helmet said.

"Aye, but we didn't," Ysir muttered. "This is the strangest place. At first, I thought it was formed by water, but there's magic woven into some of the places we've passed. Ancient magic from the days when Earth was very young.

"Native Americans view the caves as sacred," I told him, but revisiting history wasn't at the top of my list just now. I was getting more and more worried about Dariyah. Damn it to fuck. I never should have agreed to allow her to go by herself.

And then I brought myself up short. She was my mate, my partner. And her own person. She'd made a decision and didn't require permission from me or anyone else to carry it out. Besides, Dariyah was scarcely alone. I needed to give Auril more credit.

A low keening ran through the cave, growing in volume. It sounded like Banshees on the loose, but I had to be imagining it. Not the sound, but where it was coming from. Muted hoofbeats and an eerie wind were all the warning I got before a herd of ghostly riders bore down on us. Smelling of horseflesh and rot, they reminded me of a subterranean version of the Wild Hunt. Because they were dead, they rode right through us. Places where they touched my body stung, first hot, and then chill like a grave.

"Indians," Helmet said, followed by a low whistle.

Feathers, headdresses, bare torsos painted with dye, and saddleless horses kept right on coming. "Where'd they come from?" I muttered as we pressed forward.

"Once they were a hunting party that went to war against a neighboring tribe," Ysir said. "Somehow, they are tied to the magic intrinsic to these caves. If I had more time, I'd sort it out."

In their wake, the bats flew headlong into our midst, chittering a mile a minute. Titania clucked and cooed back. The lines of worry that had carved into her face relaxed, and I assumed the bats had brought good news.

"They're this way," Titania said. "And not all that far. Why couldn't I sense Auril?"

"Because the enchantment woven into the rocks is blocking everything," Ysir told her. "Someone designed this place long ago, probably for them to escape notice." He splayed his hands over a rocky outcropping, clearly searching for answers.

"Not now," I told him. "Not why we're here."

"Aye, Regent. I was merely taking a quick peek."

My throat was dry. I tried to swallow, but gave up. "We'll get closer than I'd originally planned," I croaked, "and arrange ourselves so we can attack if need be." Any worries I'd had about Pegasus sensing us had gone the way of the Dodo bird.

"Did you tell our friends we're on our way?" Ysir asked one of his bats.

"*We did,*" the bat replied.

The ghost army thundered past the other way. Did they ride back and forth endlessly? What had trapped them here and not allowed them to find peace in death? Ysir seemed to believe they were linked to the cave's power, but why hold them down here forever?

We covered the last quarter mile quickly. Finally, I

latched onto Dariyah's energy. Goddess's tits. We were linked. It should mean I always knew where she was. Not down here, though.

Ysir caught up with me. "I've been mapping this place as we've moved through it. If the warp and weft of the magic holding it together is ever severed, the whole thing will collapse."

"It's held together this long," I pointed out.

"Aye, but the tether points are wearing thin, and—"

"We'll deal with it later," I told him, my tone sharper than I'd meant.

He curled his fingers around my forearm. "Be prepared to leave quickly," he said.

"Because the cave is in imminent danger of falling in?"

"That and it's hungry. Our magic would feed it for a long while. It sucked the life out of those warriors so long ago it doesn't even recall doing it."

His words got my attention. "You're talking with whatever it is?"

"Not talking so much as exploring its layers."

"Keep an eye on it, and thank you."

Crap. The last thing we needed was one more problem. If a malevolent force lurked in these caves, it had done a stellar job restraining itself from feeding on the constant stream of humanity strolling through its halls. Perhaps twenty-first century man no longer possessed anything of value. I'd suspected as much for most of the time I'd operated Lady Luck.

"We are ready," Dariyah's voice floated through my mind. *"Hide yourselves."*

"Did he respond?" I wanted to know if Pegasus had risen to the bait.

"Maybe. No more talk."

When we'd planned this operation, I'd envisioned us in individual caverns. No need for that level of separation. We moved into the cave adjacent to where the bats indicated Dariyah and Auril were and waited. At least it got us out of the main corridor where warriors from a bygone era thundered past again. Before we left this place, I'd see if I could sever whatever tethered them to this place—if I could do it and leave the caverns intact.

Time stretched to infinity as I waited. Sweat rolled down my forehead and slicked my sides despite the constant cool temperature in the cave. Ysir walked from rock to rock, laying his hands on them as he passed by. I figured he was into his seer thing, or indulging his proclivity for mapping new-to-him places.

"What is taking so long?" Helmet muttered, mirroring my thoughts.

With less than a nanosecond's warning, a bloodcurdling neigh was joined by the reek of decomposing garbage. Pegasus had never smelled particularly fresh, but this was a big step downward. Hoofs struck granite, and I heard Dariyah say, "Took you long enough."

Something about the way the caves were structured amplified her voice.

"You have learned nothing," Pegasus shrieked and pawed the dirt-and-stone floor again.

"What would you prefer I'd have learned?" Dariyah taunted.

"Doesn't matter. I need those wings."

"In a pig's eye." Dariyah spat the words.

No reason for us to wait any longer. I ran toward the adjacent cave, hit an unexpected barrier, and almost landed on my ass. Who'd sealed this chamber? Not bothering with subtlety, I sent a beam of power forward to see if I could carve through it.

"What is that?" Titania asked.

"What's more important is who built it. Almost has to be Pegasus," Ysir said. Bolts of blue-white lightning flew from his hands as he probed. Pegasus had switched from baiting Dariyah to cursing Auril for duping him.

"Stupid bitch. I should have poisoned you like I did all the others."

"Not so dumb as all that," Auril countered. "I knocked you out and left. Has anyone told you what a shitty lay you are?"

The horse roared with rage as we shuffled through ways to defeat the barrier. Pegasus's casting was proving intransigent to our efforts.

"Got it," Ysir crowed. "Use that blade of yours."

Nothing else was working, and Pegasus would tire of verbal volleys all too soon. I drew my blade from its sheath and goosed its power until it turned into a broadsword. Hefting it with both hands, I cleaved downward and was rewarded by a ripping sound so horrendous it deafened me.

The flash and flare of magic from my three companions finished the job. We leapt through the breach and formed a semicircle around the winged horse. Except he no longer had wings. They were blackened stubs from where Ash had burned them with dragon fire. The rest of his body was sloughing off in gelatinous clumps of sticky goo that pooled around his hoofs. They were the only part of him that wasn't melting. His hoofs and the vipers his mother had used to patch his broken places.

Apparently, Medusa's snakes were immune to radiation poisoning. If I looked with my third eye, a faint glow pulsed around Pegasus. Not a magical one, but a product of the polonium.

Pegasus pranced as he took in the rest of us. Power blasted from him, covering Dariyah in something like gummy spider's web fibers. I stepped between them, and the fibers wrapped around me too. What the hell kind of enchantment was this? My power slotted with Dariyah's; we ran through combinations of elements as we struggled to defeat his trap.

Auril focused beams of power our way, but I shouted,. "Don't worry about us. Take him down. Do it now before he can leave."

"He's not going anywhere," Dariyah said. "He showed up here to take my wings since his aren't growing back."

"Never going to happen," I shot back.

An inner battle played out on Auril's expressive

features before she wrested her full attention from Dariyah and joined the others, melding her power with theirs as they sought to immobilize the no-longer-winged horse.

That had been our plan. Knock him out, deliver him to Fire Mountain, and toss him in one of the fiery pits. "Glad you're okay," I told Dariyah as we continued to chop through the cords. Some of the radioactivity must have leaked through his casting because the webbing burned like fire. When I glanced at one of my hands, bone showed through in a couple of spots.

"Okay is relative," Dariyah muttered and plucked at a part of the web slicing a path through her forearm. "What the fuck? When did he turn into a spider?"

Hoofbeats filled my ears. At first, I thought it was Pegasus changing up his prancing routine to avoid the barrage of power from Titania, Ysir, Auril, and Helmet. But then, I knew different. The horde of warriors flowed through the walls until they rode in a broad circle between us and Pegasus. Sometimes a horse and rider went through a wall before showing up again. Being dead offered a few perks.

Because Pegasus's attention had been diverted, the enchantment powering our bonds slacked off. With my blade back to knife-size, I managed to slash through enough of the ones trapping me to step out of them. I turned to Dariyah to free her, but she'd already managed it on her own.

"Ick." She kicked the useless strands to one side.

I focused some of our joined magic, instructing it to put our damaged parts back together.

"Who are they?" Dariyah nodded at the spectral figures who'd penned the horse in. Pegasus was rearing and screaming. His hoofs slapped the ground, and then he bounced back up, balancing on his hind legs.

"I don't know. They came with the cave."

"Mmph. There's a legend about an Indian scouting party who got lost in here and were turned into bats."

"That was bullshit. This is closer to the truth. They didn't turn into anything except themselves," I told her.

More gobs of flesh were sloughing off Pegasus, making splattering sounds as they hit the ground. The ghostly tribe surrounding him were whooping and hollering.

"Cut your magic," I called to everyone. "Do it slowly and see what happens."

Auril sprinted to where we stood. One by one the others joined us. I'd been right about our power becoming an anachronism. The band of warriors had formed an effective barrier around the trapped horse.

Pawing and whinnying, Pegasus brayed his displeasure. I sensed his efforts as he tried to escape with zero luck. The dirt around the horse was suddenly clear of sloughed off body parts. When a new hunk fell, it was absorbed immediately.

"We can leave," I told everyone.

"But what about taking Pegasus to Fire Mountain?" Auril asked.

"No need," Ysir spoke up. "The cave's magic is ravenous

—and starving. It will suck every residual bit of power from Pegasus's bones. It's what the tribe of warriors is for. To seek out power, hold it here, and feed it to the cave spirits."

"I'd hoped to free them," I muttered. "Not the spirits, but the warriors."

"Bad idea," Titania said. "They seem to coexist with the flood of mortals who come here, but once they're done with the horse, they'll focus on us."

"Say no more," Dariyah told her aunt.

"It's going to take all our magic to get out of here," Ysir warned.

"Let's hedge our bets and do a bit at a time." I built a hasty spell and moved us to the bottom of the ramp leading to the bat cave. Our bat guides stuck with us, even though they flinched and squeaked at the bite of magic. Titania thanked them and told them to find safe haven for the next day or two—until things settled down.

I'd picked this spot on purpose. It was still inside the cave and wouldn't give away our intentions. The next move was critical, though. Should we make a run for it up the ramp? Or should we do a joint teleport casting?

I tossed it out to the group. "Magic or no?"

My answer was five magical centers reaching for me and linking to my own. "On my count of three," I said. "One. Two. Three."

Power blasted through me like high-voltage electricity. In this case, it was still tinged with radioactive fallout from Pegasus. Maybe it gave us the edge we needed, but we broke free. A robust force attacked our casting, clearly intent on holding us in place, but we were too many and too powerful for it. Between it pummeling me and the radiation, I could have gone ten rounds with a gorilla and felt better.

We ended up in the middle of the vast wilderness that was part of the national park. No reason to remain linked or blow through scads of magic. As we disentangled from one another, I felt like cheering.

"Didn't come out quite as we'd planned," Dariyah said.

"Nay, but success is success," Auril told her.

"I'd have liked it better if we'd stuck around to make certain the horse was completely absorbed," Ysir tossed out.

"Some things require a leap of faith," Titania said. "It's past time to return to Faery."

It was. After everyone left, I closed my arms around Dariyah. "All's well that ends well, eh?"

"Ending well is relative," she said tartly. "If we really ended Pegasus, Medusa will show up damned quick with her magic set to Mach 10."

"One problem at a time."

Dariyah nodded. "True enough. Let's make a quick stop so I can reassure Midnight I'm still alive, and then we'll be back in the thick of it." She glanced at her abraded hands; they were healing but not as quickly as I'd have liked. The same held true for my wounds.

"I have a lot of questions," I said.

"Such as?" She set a spell in motion that dropped us in her mostly empty living room.

"For starters, you and I visited those caverns. I don't know about you, but I never sensed anything magical there before. To hear Ysir tell it, the power woven in with the cave system is old."

"Maybe it's particular." Dariyah shrugged. "It might lie low when the place is crowded with tourists. Could be the warriors only ride after the place closes."

"Or perhaps they only ride when they're summoned." I exhaled sharply. Some things were destined to remain mysteries, and this was one of them.

Midnight streaked through a window and clawed his way up Dariyah's body until he was snuggled in her arms. She held him, crooning wordlessly. I placed my arms around them both, grateful for a few moments of peace. Her wings unfurled, and she folded me into their feathers. The sensation was unique, sensual, and full of everything we meant to one another.

"I love you," I murmured.

"Me too," she said and glanced up until she met my gaze. "Time to go, huh?"

"Past time to quote Titania." I let go of Dariyah and went to tip more kibbles into the cat's food bowls. Our next stop was the stairs under Lady Luck. Hand in hand, we walked into Faery.

"It always used to feel like coming home when I left Earth," I said.

"And now?"

"I'm wondering what fresh hell happened while we were gone."

"Faery is still home," she pointed out.

"You're right. It is. I was just feeling sorry I can't whisk you away and—"

"I want that too." She offered an engaging grin. "Maybe if we both wish hard enough..."

"Nah. We still have a war to win."

"But we will. Win it, that is."

"How do you know?" I asked. "Did Auril's seer genes take root?"

"Oh god, I hope not. We'll win because we're the good guys."

"Reason enough for me."

The Midnight Court came into view. Everyone raced forward, all talking at once. I snapped back into regent mode. This was my land, and these were my people. "What's happened?" I asked.

"Gorgons have been sighted." Ysir narrowed his eyes. "And the Unseelie are back."

"Didn't take them long to regroup," I muttered.

"Do we strike or wait?" Helmet demanded.

I strode toward Auril's makeshift altar. "We plan. This war will not continue indefinitely. We will find a way to rid our land of usurpers once and for all."

Faery strode through a gash in the ether. "Oberon is back again," she announced. "We need to do something about him."

"Why?" I countered. "He seems like the least of our problems even if he is a thorn in your side."

"One dilemma at a time." Dariyah echoed my words from earlier.

Motioning everyone forward, I called court into session. All of them. Faery's court, the Midnight Court, and our particular one, court of the fallen. Except we wouldn't remain fallen.

I'd make certain of it.

CHAPTER FIVE, DARIYAH

I flexed my hands to get the healing magic flowing more effectively. Radiation was a big unknown, but I was gradually expelling residual bits. They felt different exiting my body, like glass shards with spines. The radioactive isotope hadn't appeared to slow Pegasus down, except he'd been losing chunks of flesh at an alarming rate. We hadn't had the luxury of hanging around to see whether his innate ability to heal himself would outstrip the relentless march of destruction.

I had a feeling the answer was no.

In a very distant corner of my mind, I felt sorry for him. He'd been a sad sight with his burned wing nubs and once-proud body eaten up from the inside. Radiation killed by instituting massive cell die-off. Assuming what I'd read was correct, Pegasus had absorbed enough polonium to knock off pretty much anyone—magical or not. Magic will regenerate most mutilation, but when there's too much destruction, no one's power can keep up with the damage.

I'd do well to save my pity for someone deserving of it. He'd meant it when he said he had dibs on my wings. They'd be a match because of our shared blood. I hadn't had them long, but they were a part of me; my magic was woven into them. A chill marched down my spine, adding to the creep factor of the departing radiation. Instead of losing myself in what-ifs that hadn't come to pass, I should be paying closer attention as Cyn and Ysir sketched out our next moves. I'd been nonplussed to hear the Unseelie had returned so quickly. Medusa hadn't lost any time, either. And I didn't care much for Oberon skulking around.

Had the dragons been successful knocking out their world? So far, no one had posed that question. Presumably, the two dragons Ash had stationed here would know. I waited for a natural break in Cyn and Ysir's presentation and strode forward.

"What happened with the Unseelie's world?" I asked the dragons.

"Gone." A satisfied rumble laced into his words.

"Gone as in vaporized?" Cyn asked. "Or gone as in everyone who lived there is no more?"

"The second one," the gold dragon replied.

"It was simpler," the red chimed in.

The way they tag-teamed their information reminded me of the dragon seers. "Did you lose any dragons?" I asked.

They looked at one another and clacked and chirped a

few times. I really should make an effort to learn their language, and I would once I wasn't up to my eyeballs in shit.

"We are not certain," the red replied.

"Aye, 'tis a question for Ash," the gold confirmed.

"At least it explains why the Unseelie are back here so soon," Ysir said.

No kidding. Whoever managed to escape had nowhere else to go. My mind had been wandering during the first part of the discussion, but it wasn't anymore. If someone had forwarded a guestimate of the numbers ranged against us, I'd missed it.

"Is it a fair supposition that whoever is here represents all of them?" I asked.

"A reasonable guess, aye, but not a guarantee we're not wrong," Cyn replied. "We will form the same companies as before. If any are light on warriors, we can do some swapping around."

Faery, who'd been silent for a bit, said, "What about Oberon?"

"What about him?" Cyn asked.

"I want to know too." I planted myself in front of Faery. From where I sat, he wasn't much more than an annoyance at this point.

"It's a mistake to underestimate him," Faery crossed her arms beneath her breasts, crinkling the rich silk of her deep-violet robe. Gold-and-silver tresses flowed down her back. Eyes that matched the burnished metal of Cyn's had narrowed as she skirted my attempt to snare her attention.

"You're who let him go," Cynwrigg reminded her, "in exchange for pointing you in the direction of your body. At the time, you assured me he wouldn't be a problem. What changed?"

"He didn't keep his word," Faery said stiffly.

I did my damnedest not to laugh, and lost. If Titania hadn't broken out in hoots and hollers, I might have had a fighting chance. When I could manage words, I said, "This isn't especially funny, but you know him far better than the rest of us. Why did you expect he'd honor anything as prosaic as a promise?"

Mother stepped between us. "This is precisely what Oberon would want. Us at each other's throats blaming one another for his treachery. Why is he a current threat? Once we hear that part, we can do a better job planning to incorporate him into our plans."

Faery inclined her head Mother's way. "Thank you."

"I owe you," Mother replied. "You hid me from those who would have snatched the babe from my womb, and again after she was born. Now, tell us why he's a threat to us currently."

"He's begun rebuilding Dubrova—with his own magic. Because he held the land-link for so long, his enchantment slots with the land still. Not as well as before, but it will make him that much harder to oust. Plus, having any part of him bound to the castle is just plain wrong. He's also established himself on Nemia. No one lives there, so it suits his purposes."

I remembered the part of Faery accessed via the land's

single ocean. Even though Nemia's gates were submerged, it wasn't. We'd fought a battle there, and long ago it had been the sea serpents' breeding ground.

"His power won't stretch far enough to be a problem," Titania said. Her words held the ring of certainty, but I wasn't convinced. What I'd seen of Oberon suggested he was one shrewd operator.

"I wouldn't be so sure of that," Faery retorted. "Dubrova's west wing is nearly whole again. And he's constructed many fortifications around Nemia, I'm not certain the gateway is still accessible."

"Why didn't you bring this up sooner?" Cyn asked.

"How? You haven't been here."

Cyn faced her squarely. "Do you mean to tell me he's accomplished all that in the thirty hours or so since I left?"

"Not exactly. I wanted enough evidence to make certain before I brought it up."

If it had been tough holding laughter back, it was even harder not telling her she hadn't wanted to end up with egg on her face, so she'd remained silent—until she couldn't any longer. I may have failed on the laughter front, but I succeeded handily keeping my mouth shut. What mattered was she'd done the hard thing and told everyone. It indicated she had a conscience—and that she'd finally picked a side: ours.

Both Cyn and I had harbored doubts about her true intentions.

"He couldn't be doing that on his own," Titania said. "Did he and the King of Winter stop squabbling?"

"Not exactly," Faery said. "The Gorgons and remaining Shadow Lords made it clear they had to work together."

"Do you suppose Medusa knows Pegasus is finally dead?" I asked.

"Is he?" Ulane, one of the unicorns, asked.

"We believe so," Cyn told him and sketched out the bones of our recent mission.

Faery listened intently. "I'd heard whispers about a ghost tribe, but never believed them," she said. "Earth is so anemic, I wouldn't have deemed her capable of supporting sufficient magic to maintain such a thing."

"It wasn't Earth, but the cavern," I said.

"Where do you think it draws its power from?" Faery did look at me then with the full weight of her unnerving gaze.

"Eh. Good point," I murmured.

"Are the birds keeping an eye on Dubrova?" Cyn asked, prodding our focus back to more relevant matters.

"Aye, Regent," Ulane replied. "They are to report anything unusual."

"Have we heard from the serpents?" Cyn glanced around the assemblage.

"Not lately," one of the satyrs replied.

The serpents had exchanged their cozy moat around Dubrova for Faery's inland sea before the last battle. "Do you want me to check on them?" I asked, thinking it would also be an opportunity to look in on Nemia and see if Oberon truly had jimmied the underwater gates.

Mother walked briskly to my side. "I'll accompany you."

"Thanks, but I'm good." Everyone's insistence I never do anything alone grated. Before I'd revealed myself to Cyn —and found Mother—I'd done everything in solo mode.

"Me too." Mother offered a sunny smile.

"Don't tarry," Cyn said. "If anything feels off, leave. We'll return with a larger band to deal with things."

"We?" I arched a brow, still feeling irritated and wondering if he was coming too. He needed to be here completing plans for the next skirmish.

"Aye." The affirmation held a jaunty note. "We as in more of our troops. You and Auril can scout out the territory."

"I'm going with them," Faery announced.

I stifled a groan and smoothed my features into an expression I hoped was pleasant but neutral. It was a waste of effort because Faery could pluck thoughts out of my mind no matter how well I guarded them.

"We'll meet you on the far side of the glade in a few minutes," Mother told Faery and took off at a lope expecting I'd follow her.

After a brief hesitation, I did. I was being childish. We were all in this together. It wasn't about me establishing independence. I'd done that ages ago. Me being surly and out of sorts because I wasn't getting my way was ridiculous.

"Drink this." Mother met me not far from her cottage and thrust a mug into my hands. The comforting scents of cinnamon and vanilla and ginger teased my nose as I gulped the warm spiced wine. After a few swallows, I felt considerably more whole than I had since Pegasus materialized in the caverns.

"What was in this?" I asked and handed the empty container back to her.

"Something to speed your healing. Even before he was shedding radiation, Pegasus poisoned everything that got close to him. Proximity is all it takes."

"He meant it when he said he was after my wings."

"Aye. He did, indeed." Mother exhaled noisily. "The warrior band was fortuitous. I'd never scryed any indication we'd have help from that quarter."

"Did you see the rest of it?"

"Not really. And it concerns me, but there's naught I can do about it. Brynn and Goren have a few working theories. Time will tell which one pans out."

"Could you lose your seer magic?" Worry coursed through me. Mother's primary magic was future-seeing. What would happen to her if it departed?

"Not lose it. Not exactly, but it could change into something else."

Fuck. She hadn't given up her habit of talking in riddles. I crooked a couple of fingers, but it didn't help. Finally she said, "I can't tell you what I don't know."

Faery melted from nearby shadows. "If you're done squabbling, we should leave."

"We are not squabbling," Mother said sharply.

Faery waved a dismissive hand. "Fine. We still need to leave. I'm concerned about Nemia's gates."

I started to say if she was so "concerned," she could have visited them on her own, but maybe she'd been avoiding Oberon. If it was true, I didn't understand why. She should be able to squash him like a bug. That she hadn't yet made no sense to me. Unless there was something I didn't know. Something big she was hiding. It would be very like her to conceal a critical element. One that might make a huge difference in our overall war effort.

I hoped to hell she wasn't in my mind at that precise moment. I'd only recently begun to view her as a true ally, not someone to sideline and placate until we were certain of her intentions.

"Let's start with the sea serpents," I suggested to cover my inner turmoil. "Perhaps they'll know something about Nemia."

"Or Oberon," Mother said. "No love lost between them."

Faery's erstwhile king hadn't thought anyone except Fae should take up breathing space, but I'd had no idea his less-than-me list contained serpents. Had it also included dragons? That would have been the height of arrogance on his part. Not to mention incredibly short-sighted.

"Ready yourselves," Faery said. "I shall take us to the shore."

The verdant expanse of the Midnight Court faded, replaced by the noise of breakers crashing against a sandy beach. Nemia's gates were well past the breaker line and on out to sea. With their ancient stone arches sunk into the ocean bottom, they could have been there since Faery was formed.

I was still shaking off the dregs of the transport spell, disturbed by how bits of it snagged on residual globs of radioactivity, when Faery walked into the waves, stopping when they hit her at knee level. She raised her voice in the dragons' harsh language. Full of whirring noises, it sometimes sounded like a buzzsaw with bird noises mixed in.

Sea serpents and dragons had risen from the same gene pool. The only difference I could see between them was that dragons had wings. Mother moved until she stood next to me and took one of my hands. Her fingers moved in a pattern that was vaguely familiar. When she'd repeated the pattern three times, everything crashed into focus.

This was a form of language we'd developed during the years we'd been on the run when I was small. Many a time, silence had been essential, and telepathy could be intercepted. I signed back that I understood. I'd used that progression of finger motions so many times they rose to my bidding easily. Anything beyond a simple, "Yes, ma'am, I've got it," would require digging, though.

Serpents were swimming toward us. The nearest ones would crawl out of the surf in short order. Mother's fingers waggled quicker. The gist I picked up was she didn't have good feelings about any of this and to remain alert. I'd have done that anyway.

Recognizable power pricked me. Nothing threatening. Just a slight nudge. And then another, but I couldn't sort out whose it was. What was it about this particular magic that plucked at my memories? Playing the better-safe-than-sorry card, I pulled my hand out from Mother's, spread my wings, and leapt skyward. If we were about to face something, I'd rather do it from up here. Still in proactive mode, I put out a mental call for Ash. The dragon had said he'd hear me, no matter what. I wasn't so certain about that. Fire Mountain was a long way away.

Serpents were heaving themselves out of the surf. Mother had run lightly to meet them, and I remembered her swimming in the moat while they vied to see whose back she'd select. They clicked and clacked and buzzed away, all the while sending gouts of steam and smoke into Faery's clear skies.

Faery had moved off to one side, her face set in stony lines. What could she possibly be angry about? Teleporting here had been her doing, and the serpents were genuinely delighted to see her and Mother. Several had slithered to Faery, while others remained ranged around Mother, forked tongues flickering in and out as they chatted.

I was the only one who didn't know their language, and I would have given a lot to follow the gist of both conversational threads: Mother's and Faery's. Taking advantage of my aerial vantage point, I scanned the water and the shore. Circling higher, I looked behind cliffs facing the beach, intent on figuring out who'd been poking me with tiny jets of power.

I followed my visual scan with seeking magic, intent on ferreting out what was going on, but didn't have any luck. If my skills were to be believed, the only living creatures in this region were the three of us—and the serpents. Even though I felt safer in the air, I circled to land.

I was being silly. Overreactive as all get-out. It must be the residual radioactivity creating a sort of paranoia. I'd be damned grateful when I was at the tail end of this chemical poisoning episode. Once my feet were on the sand, I furled my wings and joined Mother.

"Did you see anything interesting?" she asked in a conversational voice, almost as if we'd been tourists.

"Not a thing." I shrugged and scratched the nearest serpent's scaly head. "If I had, I'd still be up there keeping an eye on it."

"The serpents told me there's something amiss with Nemia's gates. They can't pass through."

Forehead scrunched in concentration, I searched my memory banks for something important. What I'd been hunting for finally came. "The dragons. They can come and go directly into and out of Nemia. Can't the serpents do the same?"

"They say no," Mother replied. "And we certainly can't. I've tried to leave that way a time or two when my magical stores weren't in tiptop shape. It never went well."

Faery joined us. "We need to take a look at the gates. The serpents told me—"

"They told us too," Mother cut her off.

"Follow me," a large red-scaled serpent invited just before turning and lumbering into the water.

The first time I'd been here, I'd been surprised how

mindless breathing underwater was. This time, I didn't give it a second thought and plunged into the salty surf after Mother and Faery. I'd have peeked into Faery's mind if I'd had any guarantee she wouldn't notice. Like as not, she'd be on high alert for just such an incursion past her warding. So I gathered my thoughts into me and held them as close as I could.

The water was cool, refreshing, but an "ick" factor ran quiet and deep. Something had entered these waters and contaminated them until they were no longer pure. I pushed and stretched and poked and prodded and was almost certain it had to be Oberon, which made sense since Faery had fingered him as being responsible for setting up a stronghold in Nemia.

Still, something bothered me about all of this, and it ran far deeper than Mother's unease and warning.

The gates came into view. Vast stone arches, they supported polished iron gates. By rights, the gates should have devolved into rust, but they were silver and shiny. I raised a spell to make them open not expecting it to have any effect. No one was more surprised than me when they creaked open on rust-riddled hinges. Interesting the hinges had rusted, but not the gates themselves.

I dusted my hands together, pleased with myself. *"That was certainly easy,"* I muttered.

"Don't get cocky, child." Mother's comment returned me to my childhood when I'd heard that phrase a lot.

Before I loosed a flood of angry telepathy, I swam through the gates. The serpents who'd come with us followed, tails swishing. I felt, rather than saw, Mother and Faery swim through.

The same clanging sound that had held such finality last time I was here thudded as the gates swung shut. They might need a spell to open, but they closed all by themselves. A short paddle brought me to the surface. Breaking through, I spied the same beach I remembered, the one bordered with poison trees.

Faery was already on shore, pacing disconsolately. What was wrong with her? She'd barely said two words since I made the mistake of laughing at her actually believing Oberon when he'd promised to make himself scarce. As I treaded water, I looked around for Mother, but didn't find her.

"Do you know where Auril is?" I asked one of the serpents.

"Aye. She's making certain the gates will let us go when we're ready."

Jackknifing my body, I dove deep, intent on helping. She stood on the Nemia side of the gates, fingers curled around the metal staves shaking them and cursing. Bubbles issued from her mouth.

"What's wrong?" I asked.

"Stupid," she sputtered. *"I was stupid not to see this coming."*

"Mother. Focus. For once, do not talk in riddles. See what coming?"

"This whole thing was an elaborate snare. We're trapped on the wrong side."

I grabbed the bars in a different place and cycled

through several castings. My magic was different from Mother's. It had gotten us in here. Surely, it would free us. After half a dozen failures, my heart hammered. If I hadn't been in water, I'd have been panting.

Mother uncurled my hands from the bars and dragged me toward the surface. Once our heads had broken through, she spoke close to my ear. "Say nothing. Let's see if Faery was party to this, but we'll have to trick her into slipping up."

"Something is going on with her," I muttered. "I called Ash. He'll be able to get us out of here."

"If he heard you," Mother said. "Something has felt off to me from the moment Faery's spell brought us here. I'm still working on deciphering it."

"Don't wait too long. We need answers, not perfection."

Mother smiled. "That's my girl. You always had a practical streak."

We covered the remaining yards to the shore in silence. I wasn't worried. Not yet. I'd have plenty of time to worry when I'd run through my entire bag of tricks and nothing had freed us.

CHAPTER SIX, DARIYAH

"Is everything all right?" Faery asked.

"Far as I can tell." Mother offered an approximation of a smile. It didn't fool me, but Faery might not think twice about it. I had to remind myself she only looked human. That could be said of me as well, but I was far closer to all the things it meant to be human than she was.

The same orange-leafed trees reeking of poison ringed the beach. We slogged past them with the group of serpents who'd accompanied us.

"Do we have a plan?" I asked. My last trip here, I hadn't taken time to scout the place. I'd been too busy fighting.

Faery shrugged. "Oberon has been here, but I've yet to identify fortifications. I looked on both shores, and the gates opened easily enough. I may have diverted us here for nothing."

"Good to check it out," Mother said. "Long as we're here, I say we do a thorough job of looking the place over."

"How big is it?" I asked.

"Manageable. Pick a direction and run with it. We'll meet back here in an hour or so." She took off to the right. The serpents fanned out, moving more quickly than they had any right to on land, courtesy of rows of tiny feet spaced along their bellies. In a backhanded way, they reminded me of a scaled version of a giant centipede.

I waited to see which way Faery was headed and took a route that would put some distance between the two of us. I thought I'd moved past her abandoning me to Medusa when the Gorgon abducted me. Apparently, I wasn't as over it as I'd thought. I warded myself and kept a close eye out for Oberon's slimy feel. I kept expecting Faery's deposed king to pop up out of nowhere leering at me like a crazed knight jousting at windmills.

The day, which had been bright and sunny, clouded over. Soon, I peered through a thick mist rising from the ground and swirling around me. It made no sense. The dirt under my feet wasn't swampy. Maybe if I gained some altitude, I'd figure this out. Determine if it was a localized phenomenon or something more widespread. If it was the latter, we should probably forget hunting for Oberon's fortifications.

There might not be any, and even if there were the lack of any evidence so far probably meant whatever he'd done in Nemia wasn't an immediate threat. Having a few minutes to myself was welcome. I'd gone from someone who spent virtually all her time alone to constantly being surrounded by people. Even though most of them meant well, the lack of solitude was a tough adjustment.

Just Cyn and me was one thing, but it was so rarely the two of us. He'd always be Faery's regent. Perhaps one day, he'd be its king. I'd joined my life and fortunes with his knowing all that, but knowing and experiencing were different animals. I'd come up with hacks to make this work, but it didn't mean I wouldn't value my few unencumbered moments.

What was Cyn doing right now? The next spate of strategies must be in place. I hoped he was getting some much-needed rest, but he'd probably dropped in at Lady Luck. Maybe all casinos were a royal pain to manage, but that one didn't seem to do well when he was gone. Not that I'd trust much of anything to a bunch of mortals, either. When everything settled down, we'd have to take a good hard look at where we wanted our base of operations on Earth, or if we even needed to be there at all.

I stared at the ground, shocked to see a footprint in the dirt until it sank in that the lug pattern matched the boots I was wearing. Somehow, I'd walked in a circle. How in the unholy fuck had that happened? I could have sworn I'd been pressing forward in the same direction.

My feet wanted to keep right on walking, but I forced them to halt while I took stock.

Crap! My mind was all over the place. I'd meant to take to the skies and get an aerial view. Instead, I was still slogging through mist that had thickened until I could barely see ten feet in front of me. Even though it didn't exactly scream magic, what else could it be? Turning around wasn't a guarantee of anything much. Not if I couldn't walk in a straight line.

It took way more effort that it should have, but I unfurled my wings and let the breeze carry me skyward. Nemia was cloaked in mist. I couldn't even see the trees with their orange leaves, but the shoreline was visible. Turning in that direction, I flew toward distant breakers crashing on unseen sand. The mist appeared bonded with the land, but not the sea.

Odder and odder. Sea fogs weren't uncommon. Land fogs, particularly ones as widespread as this one, were rare. At first I didn't think much about nothing beneath me changing. Sometimes distances are foreshortened, but after I'd been flapping for all I was worth for maybe fifteen minutes, and the ocean wasn't any nearer, the same sense of impending doom I'd sensed at the gates washed through me.

Raising my mind voice, I called, *"Mother,"* not expecting a reply. Even though I'd figured she couldn't hear me, disappointment and fear pricked deep when she failed to answer. I tried the serpents next with the same lack of results.

Alrighty then. I was alone here. On my own. The exhilaration that had rocked through me earlier ceded to a chill uncertainty that made me shiver. Should I try to raise Faery? Eh, she was such a crapshoot, I couldn't bring myself to open that door.

A rough plan took shape. My best bet would be to teleport out of here and return with help. Flying was still new enough, I'd be better served crafting a teleport spell—one I didn't expect to work—from terra firma.

Landing was harder than I'd imagined it would be. Because I couldn't see, I had a couple of close calls where I nearly tangled my wings with trees. Luckily, the poison ones only grew near the beach. My heart thudded harder than it should have, and my breath had turned to little gasping pants. I bit my lower lip so hard I tasted blood. Kicking myself for a slow-minded fool, I switched to my psychic view. It gave me what I needed to pierce the mist and find my way to the ground.

I draped myself in a ward and pushed into the center of a grove of trees, hoping their neutrality would offer me a good launch point. I'd been in shitty situations before. Lots of them. I'd find a way out of this one.

Brave words, but the first tenet of magic is to have faith it will work. My doubts from before had to take a hike. Tree branches soughed and creaked around me, and I'd be damned if I understood why. There wasn't any wind. If there had been, it would have chased the mist away.

Collective wisdom said I couldn't teleport directly from Nemia, but I was going to give it my best shot. Not much point returning to the underwater gates. Someone—probably whoever was behind the mist—didn't want us going anywhere. Even though I was reluctant to give away my position, I called Mother's name again.

While I was at it, I dissected the feel of the mist,

searching for familiar fragments of magic. Bits and pieces tantalized me but left me grasping at straws and chasing down dead ends. Luckily, I recognized the same force that had pushed me ever deeper into the mist. Still alive and kicking, it was doing its level best to keep me from leaving.

"Piss on that," I muttered and built the strongest journey spell I could. I tried to make it bulletproof and ignited it, telling it to take me away from here. For one glorious moment, I was certain I'd broken free, but then I thumped down in the same spot I'd been, dead center in the grove of trees.

Breath whistled through my clenched teeth. Had I been close enough to try again? Each separate effort would weaken me until I was out of options. Would Nemia feed my magic? That was an avenue I hadn't explored, and I was cautious as I sent tendrils of seeking magic into the earth beneath my feet, asking the land to strengthen me.

The place had the same feel as Faery, so it should be a decent match. My tentative exploration didn't yield enough of an answer, so I opened a tiny bit more of myself.

And slammed the gates damned fast. Shit. Fuck. Damn. It was like something had been lying in wait for me to link to Nemia's inherent power. The second I offered enough of a channel, something siphoned my magic. By the grace of the goddess they didn't take much because I was ready for whoever they were.

"Show yourselves!" I shouted and shook a fist skyward. I'm up for a good fight any day of the week, but I like to see my adversaries.

My words echoed, amplified by the fog, before dying away.

An idea took shape. It was a gamble, a huge one, because if it didn't work, I truly would be tapped out. With no way to restore my magic, I'd be relegated to waiting for someone to show up and rescue me. I've never seen myself as a damsel in distress, or one in need of a bailout.

Was my brainchild a wise move? Something was skulking behind the scenes manipulating me. My thoughts, my impressions, weren't totally under my control, and it was starting to spook me.

I shuffled through several other options and kept returning to the one I had yet to test. Concern for Mother hovered, never totally leaving me be. Not that she couldn't take care of herself, but I assumed she was just as trapped as me or she'd have turned the world upside down to find me.

A distant faint booming, like native drums, caught my attention. Or maybe it was footsteps. In either case, my window of time for doing something to save myself was folding in on me. Something was coming, and I'd be stupid not to assume I was the target.

What else was here? Foolish question. I wasn't about to hang around long enough to find the answer. Or for the answer to find me.

Gathering my magic close, I built a spell—the risky one —and loosed it before I could talk myself out of it. For long, heart-stuttering moments nothing happened. I held onto my casting, breathed life into it, told it to kick some serious ass. Not the place or time for doubts, unspoken or otherwise.

A sensation of knives stabbing from all sides stole my breath, but I goosed my spell. It was all or nothing, so I gave it everything I had. This might mean I'd end up in the dark, eerie space between worlds at the mercy of whoever ran the show there, but I was well past the point of no return.

Stabbing, slashing, and jabbing intensified until tears rolled down my cheeks, and my mouth opened in a silent scream. I'd be goddamned if I'd let whoever was orchestrating this know how much they were hurting me. And then, after I'd nearly given up hope—and would have done damn near anything if only the pain would stop—Nemia shattered around me, shooting me into blackness.

It took a while before I understood I didn't hurt any longer, that I wasn't under attack because I'd escaped. The only unknown was whether I'd end up at Fire Mountain or floating in infinity forever.

My reasoning had been simple. Dragons could teleport directly to Nemia, bypassing the underwater gate system. Dragons arrived from Fire Mountain. If they could make it work in one direction, I should sure as hell be able to make it work in the other.

"One victory at a time," I said out loud to steady my jangling nerves. When I took inventory, I'd expected to find my flesh shredded, but the whole knife-thing had been illusion because my clothing didn't have so much as a rip in it.

Who in the hell possessed power that strong? Not Oberon, even on his best day. Had I been right not to call Faery? If my instincts were firing on all cylinders, the answer was yes. The worst part was I'd been almost certain she'd answer, where Mother and the dragons hadn't. What that meant was unclear, and to be fair I hadn't tested my theory.

A quick check told me I had enough magic left to make it to Fire Mountain, assuming my spell ran true and that's where I ended up. Dragons would return to Nemia with me, we'd rescue Mother, and— And what then? It still might not tell us who'd loosed the mist, or who wanted to capture me.

The list wasn't all that long. The Gorgons wanted me dead. Probably so did the Unseelie king and the Shadow Lords. I refused to entertain the possibility Pegasus had survived the band of ghost warriors or the hungry cave spirits.

"Don't forget Oberon," I mumbled. "He's not part of my fan club, either."

Mmph. The list might be slightly more daunting than I'd thought. Tough to pick a more formidable batch of enemies. Who would have guessed I was so important?

The answer wasn't long coming. Mother had known. While I wished she'd told me before I catapulted into the center of a total shitstorm, I understood why she hadn't. If I'd known, the knowledge was there for the plucking, and I might have been booted out of the game before my particular mix of skills was required.

It seemed as if I'd been floating in the chilly void for too long, but I hadn't been paying terribly close attention. At first, the absence of pain and sheer relief at leaving Nemia behind overshadowed everything. I checked in on my casting. It was still clicking along. Too bad it didn't have sliders to check my progress, but magic wasn't like a computer or a video game.

Could I change destinations mid-spell? If I hearkened back to Mother's lessons, it was bad practice. But did that mean it was impossible? I'd give this five more minutes. If I didn't see the characteristic gray edges that meant I was nearly to Fire Mountain, I'd dig around a bit and see if I couldn't alter the weave of my magic.

Faery was closer. I'd even take Earth at this point.

I counted to sixty with pauses between each number. And then I did it four more times. Scrunching my eyes, I peered around me, but all I saw was unending blackness. I'd had a mage light dialed quite low—more for company than because I couldn't see in the dark. I doused it and focused inward, separating the various threads of my journey spell.

Two of them had twisted, so power couldn't flow through them. I straightened the strands and waited while I watched the pulse of blues and violets. By all rights, what I'd crafted should have spit me out at Fire Mountain. Why hadn't it?

Yeah. And if I knew the answer, I'd be able to get myself out of this mess.

No one else's magic had snuck in. It was the first thing

I'd checked for after escaping Nemia. The journey channel felt the same, but I had to be missing something.

Today was my day for taking chances.

A quick and dirty assessment of my remaining magical stores told me if I was going to change horses, I had to do it very soon. What had been a comfortable margin when I charted a course for Fire Mountain was shrinking by the minute. Of course it was because travel spells are power hogs.

They never last this long. Counting off five minutes had convinced me I'd been drifting for at least half an hour.

Yeah. Drifting and going nowhere. I doubled up my fists, squeezing to wake myself up. Damn if I hadn't stumbled onto what was wrong. Clearly, I wasn't headed anywhere, despite the specific destination etched into my spell.

Where was the disconnect?

Knowing I'd screwed up somewhere or carried residual something-or-other from Nemia that was fucking with my spell was the wakeup call I needed. The bitter taste of adrenaline coated my tongue, and I punched the air with my clenched fists.

I'd had this same problem on Nemia with my mind wandering and difficulty focusing on any one thing. It had kept me on the ground when what I'd wanted to do was fly. I bit down on my lower lip, using pain as a focal point, and culled through my magical center. This might be one more wild goose chase, but I didn't think it would be. I'd been contaminated...somehow. If I couldn't locate the problem

—and dispose of it—I'd die out here in the middle of the void. No one would ever find me. The space between worlds didn't work like that.

I was on my second trip through all the layers of my magic, taking care to peer in all the corners and pick even the most innocuous spots apart when a subtle wrongness drew my attention. Off to one side, a tiny dart burrowed deeper almost as if it were trying to hide.

It wasn't part of me. Neither was it part of my linkage to Cyn or the dragons. Had it always been there? Was it something Mother had implanted to separate me from knowledge of who I truly was.

I squeezed my earth eyes shut and dialed my psychic vision in on the offending bit of alien magic. Alien because I was 99 percent certain it hadn't originated with me. If I plucked it out and was wrong, I could do incalculable harm.

It glowed and dimmed along with the beat of my heart just like all the rest of my power. I reached for it. It drew back.

I hesitated. If I were wrong, I'd just signed my death sentence.

"I'm going to die out here if I do nothing," I told the void. My words echoed around me. The questionable dart began to fade. Great. It was sentient. If I didn't grab it now, it would hide elsewhere, and the hunt would begin all over again.

Eventually, I'd run my magic to bedrock, and that would be the end. Of everything. Because it was the only option left, I made a grab for the dart. It slipped through my grasp. As I clawed through a curve within my magic, intent on capturing the thing, pain speared me.

A giant hand closed around my heart and squeezed. That more than anything convinced me I had to see this through. Running blind, because the dart had dived deep, I went after it, heedless of grinding discomfort starting to numb my fingers and toes.

I focused all my attention and most of my remaining magic on getting hold of the slippery little devil. Once, I had it, but it slithered from my grip. Running on sheer desperation, I caught it again and ripped it free.

Screams blasted my ears. I was so far gone I didn't realize they were coming from me as I annihilated the dart with magic, crushed it, dismantled its parts, and hurled them as far from me as I could.

There wasn't enough air. Or my lungs had forgotten how to process it. I gasped and panted and gasped some more. At least the searing pain in my chest was easing off. Had what I'd done fixed anything? Or was it one more trick to force me to blow through my power?

With no warning, my casting shattered around me, and I fell through the hot, still air of Fire Mountain. I had just enough of a grasp on consciousness to spread my wings and break my fall.

CHAPTER SEVEN, CYN

The troops had their final orders. We'd settled on three hours past midnight tomorrow night to strike because we'd launched the last skirmish at dawn. Good to keep the Unseelie guessing. Hours had passed since Dariyah left. Worry nagged at me.

A large black hawk winged my way and landed on a shoulder, talons cutting through my clothes. "Still quiet by Dubrova," he squawked.

"Thank you for keeping the watch." I stroked his soft feathers.

Ysir moved close to us. "Any sign of Oberon?"

"No," the hawk squawked again.

"So far, so good," I ventured. "But what the hell happened to Dariyah and Auril?"

"I notice you didn't include Faery." Ysir quirked a bushy gray brow my way.

"She can merge with the land. Last I checked, Nemia was part of Faery." I stopped there, unwilling to float my wariness out loud. I'd just been starting to trust her, but her insistence about accompanying Auril and Dariyah had seemed off to me.

Dawn had come and gone. No one seemed to require me here, but if I stuck around that could change quickly. "I'm going after them," I told Ysir.

"Would you like me to go with you?" he asked.

"I appreciate the offer, but if I'm not here, you should be."

Titania bustled up to us, her arms laden with dusty scrolls. "A couple more trips should finish it," she announced.

I cast a speculative glance her way.

"What?" She set the scrolls down and wiped her hands on the grass.

"Have you heard from Auril?"

The queen drew her white brows together. "Nay, and it concerns me. I've tried to reach her, but either she's an exceptionally long way away, or something is blocking my telepathy."

"Not liking the sound of any of this," Ysir snarled. Power eddied from him as he cast his own version of a seeking spell.

I reached through my link to Faery, attempting to locate her. I might not trust her, but presumably she'd been the last one to see Dariyah and Auril. No reason I could come up with for her to not still be with them.

Though I altered my magic twice, focusing first on earth and then on water, I couldn't locate Faery. My land link was in place, but the other end may as well have ended in a vacuum.

Titania's arms had been extended as she wove her hands into a series of complicated patterns to augment her power. She dropped them to her sides. "Not a sign. Anywhere. It's like when Auril was on that remote world. I couldn't reach her then, either."

Nothing we'd done had eased my concerns. Quite the opposite. Where before I'd been worried, it had escalated to something close to alarm. "I'm leaving," I said. "My first stop will be Nemia. The serpents will know something, and I can take it from there."

"You shouldn't go alone," Titania said firmly.

"Same thing I told him," Ysir growled.

"We can't all leave," I told them and scrunched my face into grim lines. "If they ran into trouble—and I'm almost certain they did, or they'd have returned by now—having all of us fall into the same trap is self-defeating. We have a battle to orchestrate. Our battalion commanders will have questions, and both of you need to oversee preparations."

Before they could launch more arguments, I fanned power around me, intent on reaching Faery's sea. I aimed for the beach rather than Nemia's gates. That way, I could summon the serpents. They'd tell me what they knew.

Either my power was unusually robust, or it was driven by anxiety. Regardless, Faery's ocean took shape almost immediately. I needn't have worried about calling the serpents. I was barely corporeal before a stream of them exited the water and surrounded me, all talking at once.

"Slow down," I said and crouched in their midst, grateful for their solid presence.

A grizzled gray serpent waited for the cacophony of voices to die down before he said, "Nemia is closed to us. The gates have been locked, and many of us are on the other side."

"You can't open the gates?" I sought verification. Such a thing had never happened before.

"Aye, Regent. They are locked, and undoing them is beyond our magic," the gray serpent replied. "We have put out a call for our dragon kinsmen. They can travel directly into Nemia, bypassing the gates."

"How long ago?" I asked.

The gray shrugged amid a rattling of scales. "We do not mark time in the same way as you, but it has been too long for my taste."

"They should have been here by now," a red serpent confirmed.

"Did you see Auril, Dariyah, and Faery?" I needed to make certain they'd even been here.

"Aye. They were the last through the gates. Auril knew they were shuttered. She stood for a long while, trying this spell and that to unlock them."

"How do you know?" I asked.

"Serpents on the other side told us. A few remained off to one side in the water watching. They said Auril and

Dariyah were so consumed by the gates, they didn't notice them."

"Can you still talk with your brothers?" Hope flickered. If we could connect with anyone on Nemia, I could determine if Dariyah was still there.

The gray serpent shook his head sadly. "Communication died away just before we called out to the dragons."

"What would you like us to do, Regent?" the red serpent asked.

"First and foremost, remain safe," I told the twenty or so serpents huddled around me. Rising from my crouch, I considered my next moves. "I'm going to visit the gates," I told them, "but I don't plan to tarry. On the off chance I recognize the binding spell and can defeat it, I will open the way into Nemia again."

"Auril and Dariyah stood before them for a long while," the gray said.

"It's a long shot," I agreed. "If it doesn't pan out, I'll head for Fire Mountain."

"We will try to reach you if dragons come to our aid," the red serpent said.

"Appreciated." I lowered my voice. "The next skirmish is slated for the early hours of tomorrow morning."

"Will we ever return to our moat?" the gray asked with the dignity of any displaced person inquiring if their wartorn home would be habitable again.

"I hope so. Much of Dubrova lies in ruins, but the moat escaped harm."

Walking among them, I shook extended forelegs, feeling fortunate to have such staunch companions.

"We can swim to the gates with you," one said.

"Better if I go alone." To avoid further discussion, I loped into the surf, propelling myself forward and then down once the water reached my shoulders. If I ran into something horrible, I didn't want to force the serpents into an unexpected confrontation.

Since avoiding anything that would eat up my limited time was critical, I warded myself and swam for the entrance to Nemia. How had the gates come to be in the first place? Nowhere else in Faery had them. Ysir probably knew. I'd have to ask him someday.

Sunk into sand and rock, the gates rose before me. Normally iron is hard for me to deal with, but saltwater muted the worst of the metal's emanations. After making certain I was alone, I jettisoned my ward and tested the gates with a shot of enchantment. They vibrated, creaking on their hinges, but didn't budge. My next effort wasn't to open them but to figure out who had spelled them shut. Every mage has a characteristic magical "signature." If I could determine who was behind this latest batch of treachery, it might help me dismantle their casting.

Once the gates were open, the serpents trapped on the wrong side would be free to join their fellows. And I'd be able to search for Dariyah and Auril. The more I poked and prodded, the more certain I became the gates were but a single manifestation of a much larger spell, something that extended through at least part of Nemia.

Snatches of Oberon wafted through, but he'd played a minor part. I dug deeper, but didn't get any closer to knowledge that would lead me to a breakthrough. Time was passing, except my sense of urgency had departed. I drifted with the water, lost in a trancelike state.

I might have remained there, certain I was doing important work, but actually spinning my wheels, if my hand hadn't brushed the gate. A shock ran up my arm and propelled me back to reality. I stroked back from the polished iron. Fuck all of this. The enchantment included a mesmerism component. A strong one. Were Dariyah and Auril lost in opium-dreams somewhere on Nemia while the spell strengthened itself by draining their magic.

Mine was more-or-less intact, but I'd had the water to buffer everything.

Convinced I couldn't do this alone, that I needed the dragons, I set a path for the shore. The serpents surrounded me again, their scaly faces reflecting hope. "You were gone a long while, Regent," one said.

I nodded. "Too long. Watch the gates. They're hypnotic and want you to think everything is perfect. They caught me up."

"How'd you escape?" the gray serpent asked, concern in his gravelly voice.

"Knocked into one of the staves. The iron pricked deep enough to break through. Move inland for short while," I told them, not trusting whether the enchantment would spread, using the sea as a medium.

I set a journey spell in motion, intent on Fire Mountain. If I had any hope of blowing that deuced spell to smithereens, I needed dragons. We'd teleport directly into Nemia, track down the source, and destroy it. How much time had I lost in la-la land? No matter if it was only a quarter hour, it was too much.

One thing was certain. Faery wouldn't have been snared in such a casting. Her power was deep, ancient, and very different from any other mage. Either she'd made a cowardly retreat when the going got tough, or she'd had a hand in what had turned to shit on Nemia.

Going there in the first place had been her idea. We'd followed her lead. Maybe not the sharpest move on our part given her previous shenanigans. Eh, it was too kind a word for whatever was motivating her. Something was. Having the land link should offer me a way to tease out whatever was driving her, but she'd hidden it so deep no one could find it.

I wanted to hurry my teleport casting along, but they unfold in their own time. I couldn't afford to burn my power down to save a few moments. Finally, grayed-out edges told me I was close. The cracked, dry earth of Fire Mountain flared into view, and I fashioned a cushion of magic to break my fall. The plain was empty; so were the skies.

I broke into a run, heedless of sweat rolling down my body, as I sought the caves. The cliffs came into view. I ran harder, breath burning my throat and lungs as I inhaled the superheated air.

Before I got to the opening, a form erupted from the

cave and ran toward me. Dariyah! I stopped dead, not believing it was her. Blinking furiously, I willed her not to be a hallucination born of the ungodly hot air currents. The closer she got, the surer I was it had to be her. Tension that had been wound to the point of exploding within me started to relax.

"But you're on Nemia," I sputtered as she catapulted into my arms. I clasped her so tight, she yelped. Backing off but not letting go, relief beyond words rocked me to my bones. She wasn't stuck on Nemia, mired in the sticky web of a hypnotic casting after all.

"I was," she corrected me. "I escaped by the skin of my teeth. It was so close, I nearly didn't make it, and I'm still sucking magic like a crazy woman from Fire Mountain's core."

"What happened?" I held her tighter.

Before she could answer, Ash lumbered to us. "How's your reservoir?" he asked Dariyah.

"Another few minutes, and I'll be good to go," she replied.

"Excellent. Let me know the moment you're full up." The dragon turned to me. "We're on our way to Nemia. The serpents need us, and I understand the gates are sealed and a mesmerism casting has the land in a death grip."

"I know. I stopped there—or as close as I could get— before coming here. Is Auril with you?" I asked Dariyah.

She unwound her arms from me and shook her head. "I'm worried half to death about her. I called and called before I left Nemia. She never answered."

"Faery?" I tried for bland, but the word emerged as a curse.

Dariyah's wings quivered. "I couldn't bring myself to call for her, so I didn't."

"Might have been wise," Ash rumbled, "but I cannot see her turning to evil."

"A better question," I said, "is why we suspect her in the first place. It's never been my go-to place for her, even when she hesitated before allowing me to claim the land link."

"We won't know until this is over," Ash said. "In the end, she will reveal herself."

"Or not," I said sourly. "She'll align herself with the winning side, and we'll never truly know."

"It doesn't matter," Dariyah murmured. "We talked about this. So long as the choice she makes in the end is the right one, the rest can slide."

I held my peace unsure if I wanted to spend eternity holding onto a land link with a being I didn't trust. The link gave her access to my magic. Not that I couldn't slam the door, but it meant I'd have to be on my guard all the time.

"We can leave," Dariyah said.

Ash turned his head and trumpeted. Ten dragons flew toward us. Who knew where they'd been before. Maybe on the far side of the mountain range gorging on wildebeest.

"Thanks for bringing reinforcements," I said.

"Did you try the gate?" Ash asked, ignoring my statement about additional dragons to back our play.

"Aye. And it caught me up in its pull. Not the gate, but the spell. I have no idea how much time I wasted in some kind of trance."

"You too, huh?" A frustrated breath huffed from Dariyah. "The damned thing even followed me into my teleport channel."

"How'd you overcome it?" I asked, all too aware I hadn't had the same experience, which might mean whatever it was had set its sights more on her than on me. Once I left, I was no longer of interest.

She screwed her mouth into a grimace. "You won't like it."

"Hurry up and tell him. Better yet, tell him *en route*." Ash's magic settled around her and me, and we were yanked into a group casting with all the other dragons.

I nudged Dariyah. "I need to know."

She shook her head as if to dispel something wicked. "A dart had taken root in my magic. I figure it came from my time on Nemia since I wasn't having problems focusing before that."

"A dart," I repeated. "Invaded your magic."

"It's what I said, isn't it?"

"Aye, but who attacked you? And how'd you escape?"

Another labored breath rushed through her. "The second question is easy. I couldn't teleport out of there. Not from the Nemia side of the gates. After trying and failing, I thought about the dragons who come and go and set my destination for Fire Mountain. It was my last resort, and by the grace of the goddess, it worked.

"You asked who attacked me this time. The list of possibilities is long." She held up a hand, but I closed mine around it.

"Never mind. It was a rhetorical question. Do you think they did the same thing to your mother?"

"I'm certain of it." She turned her green-eyed gaze full on me. "I've been hunted before, but this time was worse by a factor of a hundred."

"Oberon?"

Dariyah shook her head. "I tried to locate him, but all I found were wisps. Like if he'd been there, it was a while ago."

"Same."

"It gets worse," she muttered. "I was warded. Whatever did this drilled right through my warding."

"Were you warded the whole time? Think. This is important."

She closed her teeth over her lower lip, biting hard enough to leave an impression. "Mmph. Good point. I wasn't when Mother and I stood by the gates and cycled through spells trying to get them to open."

"So, somehow, the mesmerism casting is tied to whatever is holding the gates shut. Surely, whoever did all that knows dragons don't require the gates." I slapped my forehead with my open palm and turned to Ash. "We could be walking right into a trap."

The dragon chuckled, blowing steam all over me. "Already thought of that," he informed me. "Why bait a snare, one where only dragons can tread, without an overarching purpose? Dragons have made a big difference so far in this war. If someone figures they can knock out a few of us, they're in for a rather unpleasant surprise."

"Does immortal for you mean you truly can't die?" Dariyah asked.

"Something like that," Ash answered her.

"We're nearly there," one of the dragons trumpeted.

"Onto my back, both of you," Ash instructed Dariyah and me.

"But I can fly," she protested.

"Your wings didn't save you from being captured," Ash pointed out. "Besides, you'll be within my warding—and your own—riding me. Dragons do not care for passengers. Get on before I change my mind."

I clambered up his scaly hide, chopping holes in my trousers. Dariyah spread her wings and flapped into position in front of me. She was no sooner settled than the journey channel broke into pieces, and we flew through Nemia's thick, sticky air.

"Many serpents are stuck on this side," I murmured.

"Aye, and they know we are here," Ash said.

The rumble of an earthquake and rockfall grew louder fast. Whatever we'd flown into, we'd be in the thick of it immediately. I'm not the praying sort, but I offered up a request to Danu to see us out of this so I could get back to Faery to lead us into war.

Lightning forked across the thick clouds. Rain spat from above, an icy sleet that pattered off Ash's scales. The next explosion nearly unseated me.

Ash trumpeted loudly and flew faster. I wanted to ask where we were going, but I'd find out soon enough.

Between the earth erupting below us and the skies emptying out from above, this couldn't last long. No one could keep up that kind of outpouring of power. Fire blasted from Ash's open jaws. It carved through the thick soupy clouds, not for long, but Gorgons came into view with Shadow Lords riding them.

"It's bad," Dariyah mumbled, "but at least we know what we're up against."

Ash's hind feet touched down on something I couldn't see, so I switched to my psychic view. A jagged mountain range with us balanced on a precipice came into view. The other dragons were close. I saw them through my third eye, but I also saw Gorgons. Worse, they'd brought company.

"Harpies." The word curdled on my tongue. At least there were only three of them, and they were incapable of producing more of their ilk.

"Ready your magic," Ash screamed. "Keep up a barrage until they're finished."

If a method existed to kill off Harpies, I wasn't aware of it, but the dragon was truly ancient. If anyone could manage it, he could.

The sky lit with fire. Dariyah leaned one way and tucked her wings out of the way. I leaned the other; we loosed volleys of destructive magic as quickly as they formed.

At least she was with me. I was worried about Auril,

but Dariyah was my heart. My soul. My life. Determined to kick the fuck out of every evil thing ranged against us, I redoubled my efforts. The air thickened with smoke, ash, and flames until I was gasping around the fumes.

Low booms rocked our perch. Ash unfurled his wings and shot off our ledge like a rocket in the nick of time. The entire mountainside burst upward, followed by magma hurtling high into the air.

A low keening moan from Dariyah alarmed me. "What is it?"

"Mother," she cried. "Mother's down there somewhere."

CHAPTER EIGHT, DARIYAH

Faery had volcanoes. It was news to me, but then I didn't really know much about the land that had been barred to me until recently. Perhaps they weren't volcanoes after all. A crafty earth-based mage could create the illusion of them. Or maybe Faery had gotten off her duff and decided to help. Except the ongoing blasts cut both ways. We weren't any better off than our enemies.

Usually, I opt for independence, but I was grateful to be astride Ash in the midst of explosions that kept right on shooting molten rock all around us. The dragon bucked and wove and avoided the worst of things. Remaining on his back required attention—and judicious shots of magic.

Cyn and I expanded our ward until it met the edges of the dragon's, strengthening it. So far chunks of rock, even big ones, had bounced off our protective shielding.

A bloodcurdling shriek snapped my head up and to the

right. A Harpy was headed right for us. I'd read about them, but never seen one. Confronted by the sight, I'd have been damned glad to leave my knowledge in the cerebral realm. Predatory monsters, half bird, half woman, this one had wispy silver-and-green hair and eerie red eyes. Her torso was bare; feathers began at stomach level and thickened as they descended to cover her legs and feet. Long, sharp ruby talons graced her fingers and toes.

I'd thought something like a Harpy would be troll-sized, but she couldn't have been more than five feet tall, with a wingspan equal to her height. Hard to take anything slightly smaller than the average human seriously, but something about her fascinated me.

"Do not look." Cyn reached around me and covered my eyes.

"Stop that." I batted his hand away, but he didn't move it.

"She or her sisters are who trapped you earlier," he said. "Me as well. Don't you recognize the feel of her? The attraction?"

I shook my head to clear it and achieved a moment when cobwebs receded. My case of fuzzy-brain had been growing without me even knowing it. "The trance came from them?" I sputtered.

"Aye. The moment I felt that one's power, I knew. She's Aello. The other two are Ocypete and Celaeno."

"Sea storm, swift flying, and dark storm," I translated and ducked from beneath Cyn's protective fingers.

"Doesn't matter what you call them," Cyn growled.

"They're soul stealers. They mesmerize you, fly close, and suck your soul out through your mouth."

"Ewww. That wasn't in anything I read." I quit there. The nasty truth was I hadn't read all that much, a deficiency I planned to rectify—someday.

Aello's burnt-orange wings flapped so fast they were a blur as she closed on Ash. Her hands were clasped in front of her, talons laced together. The dragon opened his mouth and inundated her in flames. She kept on flying. From my vantage point, it didn't appear any of her had caught fire.

Damn. If dragon fire didn't do it, what would?

I altered the weave of our warding, hoping to protect myself from falling back into la-la land. Mother was here somewhere. I should leave the relative safety of the dragon's broad back and go look for her. Maybe if I were on the ground, I'd be able to sense where she was.

Didn't work for me last time, I reminded myself, but it wasn't much of an excuse.

"Ash. It's been far too long," The Harpy purred in accented Old Gaelic, her voice like finely-woven silk.

"You can skip the pleasantries. Why are you here?" The dragon feinted to one side and hit another part of the Harpy with fire. Her backside didn't start smoldering, either.

"To help. Why else?" She flashed a sunny smile displaying pointed teeth. This was the gift that kept on giving. If hypnosis didn't do it, did she go after you with her chiseled incisors?

I'd finally hit on a combination of magic in our warding

that left me clearheaded. Hopefully, it would last. The Harpy probably wasn't canny enough to switch up the frequency she used to reel in the unsuspecting. She'd never had to. Victims fell at her feet like kewpie dolls.

"Help who?" Ash roared. In a surprisingly acrobatic move, he rolled to one side and caught the Harpy's hair in his back talons. Aello shrieked and ripped at her hair, but Ash's hold was solid.

Cyn spun bands around her to quiet her flailing limbs—and ensure she couldn't get away. She'd been scrabbling at the dragon's hind legs with her ruby claws; after Cyn was done, she couldn't reach Ash any longer.

"Either you talk, or we're leaving," Ash pronounced.

"Ha! You wouldn't desert your fellow dragons. It's not like you."

"Oh, we wouldn't be gone long," he rumbled, showering her with ash and smoke. "Doesn't take much time at all to drop you into Fire Mountain's caldera where you can burn forever. Think about it. Each time your magic reanimates a body part, it will burn anew. The agony will be exquisite. And endless."

I hadn't seen this side of the dragon's leader, but it didn't surprise me. It shed light on Faery's harsh edges. I'd been correct about her not interpreting events the same way I did.

"But we're friends," she screeched. "Old companions."

"We were never friends," Ash corrected her. "Not after you and your sister stole a dragon egg."

"It was a joke. A prank. We gave it back."

"Only because we chased you and forced the issue."

"We wanted a pet dragon. We would have been kind to him." The Harpy kicked against Cyn's bonds.

"Dragons are no one's pets," Ash shouted. "Enough. We are done here."

I felt him drag power into a journey spell.

"Stop! I'll tell you," Aello cried. "It's the Gorgons and Shadow Lords."

Ash paused his nascent casting. "Who else?"

"The Unseelie king. He never forgave that bitch who walked out on him."

"Watch your tongue," I carped. "That bitch is my mother."

"I don't care whose mother she is," Aello spat with a surprising show of spirit considering we'd cornered her.

"Who else?" Ash pressed. "You're not done."

"Infernals," she snarled. "Tantalus and Ixion. Maybe Hades. Loose me, dragon. I would leave this place."

"Who made the earth erupt?" The Harpy only thought she was done. Ash had other ideas.

"Shadow Lords."

"How did they access Faery's core?"

"Give it a rest," the Harpy shrieked. "Let me go."

"Your fate remains in my talons," he reminded her.

She wriggled in his grasp. "The two kings," she gritted out, "did something."

Two kings? Pretty much had to be Oberon and the King of Winter. Except Oberon wasn't exactly a king any longer.

"I have to go look for Mother," I told Cyn, pitching my voice low.

"Wait until this plays itself out," he whispered back.

A beam of red light laced with dragon magic augured from Ash into Aello's head. For long moments, it flickered and played about her strange features, illuminating one part after another. Skewered by his power and Cyn's, the Harpy hung limp in his talons. With zero warning, he opened his claws and dropped her.

Before she could recover, her head exploded, showering everything below her with bits of bone, brain, and gristle. I'm grand at asking the hard questions, so I piped up, "Is she dead?"

"Nope," Cyn said. "She can regrow any body part, and quicker than you'd imagine. He reeled in the enchantment that had helped immobilize her.

"They'll leave," Ash said.

"How can you be certain?" Cyn asked.

"Because they care more for themselves than anyone else. They may have been recruited to fight us, but when the going gets rough, they'll save their own hides."

"It's exactly how the Unseelie used to operate," Cyn informed him. "Better hope the save-your-ass gene runs deeper in Harpies than it does for the Sidhe."

Ash propelled us through the murky skies. The explosions had slowed, and my brain was working overtime. I didn't care for any of the conclusions crashing through me. No matter how I spun the facts, though, I came back to the same sticking point.

"Was all this, including the locked gates, a trap for Mother and me?" I asked. Maybe if I tossed it out there, Cyn or Ash would have a different take.

"Who else?" Ash trumpeted and switched to telepathy. *"You are the lynchpin in this war. If you aren't here, it ensures victory. But not for us."* He overflew the groves of trees with their poison orange leaves and landed on the shore. A brisk bugle brought the other dragons. Soon they joined us on the ground.

"We seem to be alone again," Cyn said. "I can't sense the Gorgons or the Harpies."

"And the Shadow Lords have gone to ground," Ash said. "Aello understands if she doesn't vanish and stay gone, the next time she sees me I'll make good on my threat."

The glitter of strong magic jabbed into my eyes, so powerful it gave me an instant headache. Faery dragged herself out of the surf, hair and clothes drying almost immediately.

"I knew that would chase them away," she announced and dusted her hands together.

Cyn jumped down from the dragon. I was right behind him. "Where have you been?" His voice was like stone. "And why did you bring Dariyah and Auril here in the first place?"

Before she could answer, I shouted, "Where is Mother?"

Faery shifted her unusual gaze from Cyn to me and back again. "No thank-yous? I do not have to answer either of you."

I grabbed hold of Cyn's arm, but he ignored my cautionary touch. Because it hadn't worked, I breathed the word, *"Don't,"* into his mind.

Sea serpents who'd been trapped on the wrong side of the gate slithered toward us and joined the dragons, trumpeting and bugling their thanks.

Oblivious to everything, Cyn planted himself in front of Faery. "You said Oberon had carved out a niche here. It's why Dariyah and Auril went with you. To cut him off before he established any kind of toehold anywhere on Faery."

Breath hissed from him. "They trusted you, and look where it got them. Dariyah was nearly lost in the void between worlds. Auril is missing, and—"

"Nay. Not missing, but it was nip and tuck for a while." Mother's voice was raspier than usual.

I spun and ran toward her bedraggled form stumbling toward us. Dirt was caked in her hair. Her skirt and tunic had long rents, and blood dripped from deep cuts in her face, arms, and hands. Heedless of the muck clinging to her, I hugged her close and poured power into her.

"My turn to replenish your magic," I murmured as I held her close. She didn't fight me. Shuddering breaths rolled through her, but she was breathing. Damn it. I'd never been so relieved she was tough as old shoe leather.

"I'm good for now." She straightened and continued toward the dragons and Cyn, far steadier on her feet than she'd been.

"Where were you?" I asked.

"When I understood I couldn't leave—and I tried, probably too many times—I took what was left of my magic and sank deep into the land. Faery found me and told me to stay put. That she'd figure something out."

"Why didn't you tell me where she was when I asked?" I demanded, aiming my words at Faery.

"She could have moved. Auril was never one for following directions." Faery looked askance at me.

"You never answered me." Cyn hadn't moved from his spot toe to toe with Faery.

"Nor do I plan to," she retorted and thumped his chest with an index finger. "You are regent, but I am the land. You answer to me, not the other way around." Her eyes narrowed to slits, and I swear she drew herself up a few inches taller than she'd been before. "You stopped trusting me. I suggest you begin again."

"Trust has to be earned. When you saw events were running off the rails, why didn't you intervene?"

"I did. I was working on the gates. They're operational again. It took a while."

"When did you discover they were locked?" I asked and focused my full attention on her. At the point we'd split up on Nemia's shore, Faery had announced blithely that the gates opened easily enough, which was true. They had, but once we were on the Nemia side, they'd become resistant to efforts to reopen them. Mother and I knew. We'd spent time throwing variations of power at them to get them to yield.

"A serpent found me and told me. He'd tried to return through them, and discovered the way was blocked."

One of the green serpents glided toward her. "I appreciate your efforts, my lady. Even if they weren't successful until now."

"See?" she hissed in Cyn's face and disappeared amid a swirl of shining light.

If I'd known a serpent was about to corroborate her story, I'd have draped a truth net over him, but I was too late. Were they lying? No way to tell. But the question of the hour was why everything Faery did got my hackles up. I either needed hard proof, or to move beyond whatever was sticking in my craw.

"The gates are truly open now," another serpent announced as he (she?) waded from the surf. "I just checked. Not standing open, but the usual spell unlocks them."

I screwed my face into a grimace. Of course they'd open. Whoever was behind this had failed to capture me. Mother was a bonus, but I'd been the primary target. And I had enough allies fanned out around me to discourage anyone from wasting magic perverting Nemia's gates.

"We'll fight another day," Ash announced. He'd been talking with the dragons and serpents in their unique language with its clicks and clacks and whistles.

"Time to leave," Cyn agreed.

The serpents turned and plodded toward the surf. Their transition from awkward to graceful as they went from land to sea was a delight to watch. "Shall we join them?" I asked him.

"Soon," he replied and walked toward the dragons. "Can we secure Nemia? Make certain it doesn't become a bastion for our enemies?"

Ash nodded. The motion made his scales jangle in a musical discord that was surprisingly soothing. "We were just talking about that. The one to barricade it would be Faery."

"I'll be sure to mention it next time I see her," Cyn muttered.

I shared his frustration and his suspicions, but he had to either move on them or leave them behind. Just like me. I gestured Mother close and crafted a journey spell, so I'd have it at the ready once we passed the gates and hit the far side.

"Go ahead," Cyn told me. "I'll catch up soon."

If we hadn't had such a large audience, I'd have asked what he was doing, but he didn't require permission from me. Mother leaned against me, and we walked into the sea. Sure enough, the gates opened easily. We swam through, and I kindled the casting to return us to the Midnight Court.

"Did Faery really rescue you?" I asked, curious to hear more about Mother's problems on Nemia.

"Nay, I rescued myself. She merely found my hiding spot."

The glade of the Midnight Court bloomed around us. Mother laid a finger over her mouth in the universal sign to keep quiet and led the way to her humble cottage. Once we were inside, she spoke a power word that must have cost her, but a ward snapped into being.

"It's a sound shield," she explained and sank into a chair. "Hand me the mead, would you?"

After rustling in a cupboard, I came up with a promising bottle and handed it over.

"Thanks," she said and took a long slug before offering it to me.

I pulled up the other chair and sat across from her.

"You escaped?" Mother narrowed her eyes my way.

Nodding, I said, "Barely. Someone had implanted a barb in my magic. I have no idea where it came from, but once I ferreted it out and destroyed it, I ended up on Fire Mountain."

"It almost has to have come from Faery," Mother muttered.

My eyes widened. With all my mental meanderings, that possibility hadn't occurred to me. "I suppose you're right, but why would she do that if she's not working for the other side?"

"Lots of reasons." Mother's tone was acerbic. "You refused to let her use your body."

"But she has her own."

Mother flapped a hand. "Details. At the time, she didn't. Plus, you're Cyn's mate. She might have a proprietary interest in him since he now holds the land link."

"Was she possessive of Oberon?" I took the bottle back

and drank, enjoying the heat and bite of the alcoholic liquid as it passed down my throat.

"Aye. Quite. But he and Titania had a marriage of convenience. Oberon's heart was never in question. If he gave any of it to anyone, Faery won. The situation with Cynwrigg is quite different. His first allegiance is to you, and I'm not sure the land can forgive him for that."

I licked at suddenly dry lips, stunned by the implication. "So she could be working against me all by herself, not necessarily in league with the Unseelie and all those other bad guys?"

Mother nodded. "Exactly. The way I see things, she took advantage of the Harpies and the trance they chucked over Nemia to bend fortune to her liking. If it meant the end of you, she wouldn't have shed a single tear."

"Aren't I elemental to winning the war? What am I missing here?"

"You are," Mother agreed. "What you're missing is Faery doesn't care who wins. She'll cozy up to whomever ends up on top. To her way of thinking, the land will endure. The only place she was vulnerable was when Oberon—a true king of Faery—held the land link. She can sever anyone else's claim to her."

"So if, for example, she ceded the link to the King of Winter, she could take it back at any time?" I wanted to make certain I understood.

"Yup." Mother pushed the bottle back my way. "Finish this and then tell me how to find that in-between place where you replenish your power."

I tipped the last few swallows into my mouth. "She doesn't think anything like we do, huh?"

"Nay, she doesn't. Faery's first concern is for the land. It's why she didn't give a damn when Dubrova fell. Her second concern is for those who live on Faery since their combined power supports hers. Beyond that, who rules is incidental."

"Does Cyn know all that?"

Mother lifted her shoulders in a small shrug. "You can ask him. I'm not sure. He should, but Oberon did a piss-poor job preparing him to be regent."

"Because he was planning to slot that cousin of his into the job," I mumbled.

"There was that. I'd almost forgotten Aedan. Now, how do I find the in-between?"

"Mix fire and earth and send it here." I rattled off coordinates to my favorite watering hole. Before the words were completely out of my mouth, Mother was gone. Her warding, the one that had protected our conversation from prying ears, dissipated gradually.

I should get up. Find Ysir and Titania, but my head slumped to one side. I shut my eyes. Not for long, I promised myself. Just enough to rest them. I tapped into Faery's magic and let it fill me while I took a brief time out. Maybe I should have joined Mother in the in-between, but Faery's well didn't feel tainted. Even she couldn't ensure I drank from a different vein than everyone else in her land, so extracting power from her core was safe enough for now.

I'd meant my time out to be brief, but Cyn's hearty, "There you are," woke me.

For the second time, a sound shield descended. "We need to talk," he said, not sounding nearly as genial, and waited for his spell to reach full strength.

9

CHAPTER NINE, CYN

My first stop before the Midnight Court had to be Faery's lair deep beneath the land. We needed to hash some things out. If I didn't like her answers, or worse, if she were evasive, I'd sever the land link myself. In many ways, it was an intricate, intimate bond, and I wasn't willing to have her that close to me the way things were.

Before, I'd threatened to walk out and let her deal with the Unseelie horde on her own. It might come to that, but I'd been angry. I was still annoyed, but my conflicted feelings ran deeper than that. I was disappointed and sad there was a need for her and I to clear the air. If I ran with my sadness and sense of betrayal, I'd probably get further than if I let my temper take over.

"What do you have in mind?" Ash's deep voice snapped

me out of my thoughts—and my half-constructed journey spell took a hike.

I turned to face the dragon. "You probably already know, so why ask?"

"Because you're making a mistake."

I decided to play dumb. "About which thing?" Before he could answer, I went on, "Whatever happens, I'm doing this for me, not for Faery. I have to trust in her good intentions toward my realm, or I can't keep up my end of our partnership. If I can't find a sliver of honor, of respect for her role in preserving the land that bears her name and her spirit, I won't be able to do my share, either."

An old saying ran through my head, and I gave voice to it. "A house divided against itself cannot stand."

"A mortal said that." One of the dragons blew steam along with his words.

"Aye, one by the name of Abraham Lincoln. As mortals go, he was one of the better ones. Regardless, the sentiment behind it is true. Faery and I must be in better accord. Perhaps she didn't talk to Oberon during the years he reigned, but she needs to talk with me. I don't have to know everything, or even the majority of what drives her, but we have to do better than we are."

"The years after Oberon left when he held fast to the lank link were hard on her," Ash said in quieter tones.

"They were hard on us all," I reminded him. "She doesn't get to be any more special—or any more wounded —than anyone else."

The dragon shook himself from the tip of his tail

upward in an undulating wave of scales. The golden tones caught sunlight filtering through the dispersing clouds. The interior of Nemia was a jumbled mess, but the shoreline hadn't changed except for a couple of the poison-leafed trees that had become uprooted.

"When is the next battle?" Ash asked me.

"Three hours past midnight, but depending on how things go with Faery, that might change."

"Why would it?" another dragon asked.

"Aye," a third chimed in. "You are too far downstream with your plans to derail them."

I cocked my head to one side. "Explain."

"What he means," Ash stepped in, "is you selected a path." He stopped for a moment before starting anew. "Actually, Auril chose for all of you when she decided to seduce Pegasus. The wheels she set in motion that day must turn until there is no more momentum."

"What happens if they don't?" I asked.

"Evil will win, and the trajectory of every magical creature will be permanently altered."

"It could happen anyway," I pointed out. Auril's vision had suggested what needed to happen, but it hadn't come with guarantees of success.

"The gods might come to our aid," Ash said, "but none of them will lift a finger if you've given up."

"I can't not talk with her," I told him.

"You could ignore her until this is done," he suggested.

I shook my head. "Nope. So far, she abandoned Dariyah when Medusa showed up. She's been vocal about her dislike for her, and she just dumped her here in Nemia and didn't lift a finger to rescue her." I blew out a tense breath. "While I can look past Faery treating me like a second-class citizen, I cannot forgive her cavalier attitude toward the woman I'm mated to."

So long as I was on a roll, words fell from my mouth. "I don't trust her, and I need to."

"You do know she heard you," Ash pointed out.

"Maybe," I countered. "If she was listening. The consensus is we're not important enough for her to bother with."

"She might surprise you," Ash said. "Let me know about tonight's battle. We will bring the same allies we did last time."

I bowed low. When I straightened, I said, "Many thanks for your aid. It's deeply appreciated."

"If Faery fails, we won't be far behind," Ash said, "so our assistance isn't exactly altruistic."

I'd forgotten that part, the wrinkle about good magic unraveling. It was painful to think about, which was probably why I'd set it aside. "I'll do the best I can to establish a workable détente," I told him and meant it. Not the response he was angling for. What Ash wanted me to do was drop the whole thing, but it wasn't going to happen.

Before he took another shot at my resolve, I walked into the water and crossed through the gates. I'd already told the serpents to lie low, so I didn't need to stop and talk with them. Kindling a travel spell, I aimed for Faery's lower levels.

My spell ran true, but then most of them do, and I walked the last few hundred feet into Faery's depths.

"Figured you'd show up." Her voice vibrated against my ears, even though I couldn't see her. One more twist in the circular tunnel, and we ended up face-to-face.

"Why'd you think so?" I inquired, mostly to buy myself thinking time. She and I would only have this talk once, and I hoped for a workable outcome. The way Ash had been carrying on, it seemed he expected me to throw all Faery's failings in her face and stomp out.

Appealing as that approach was, it would buy me less than nothing.

"I am not in the habit of explaining myself," she informed me.

"How did you and Oberon get by all those years?" I asked.

"We rarely talked. When we did, he acquiesced to my demands."

I narrowed my eyes. "You only thought he did," I said, keeping my tone mild. "Oberon marched to his own drummer."

Faery shrugged her broad shoulders. "What difference does it make. We found a way of working together."

"Until he sold you out," I reminded her.

"If you're referring to his alliance with the Unseelie, they used to live here too."

I thought about what her words meant and picked my way forward. "Did you miss them once they departed?"

"What kind of question is that?" she demanded.

"A simple one."

"Of course I missed them," she said. "They were part of me in the same way the Fae are. Or unicorns or fauns or satyrs or birds."

Interesting. "When Oberon forged an alliance with the King of Winter, were you hopeful the Unseelie would return?"

Faery nodded, an unreadable expression on her gaunt face. "If he hadn't invited all those others, I could have been whole again."

At least it explained why she'd overlooked the King of Winter's incursion into her lands. Still proceeding cautiously, I asked, "Why did you lead Dariyah and Auril into Nemia?"

"To see if Oberon had been there."

Her response was too pat, rather like someone protesting their innocence in the face of evidence to the contrary.

"That explanation might work," I told her, "but not with me. You must have sensed the Harpy intrusion and known they'd woven a mesmerism casting, but you didn't warn either Dariyah or her mother."

Faery tossed her head back. "If it hadn't been for Auril, the Unseelie never would have left."

"So you blame her?"

"Who else?" Faery's nostrils flared. "I've always liked Auril, and I helped her when she was with child, but I never forgave her, either."

"And Dariyah?" I arched both brows.

"Pfft. That one. And then you had to go and choose her as your mate. Why couldn't you have selected someone more fitting?"

"What's wrong with her?" I kept my tone even. No need to go into our joining being preordained somehow.

"She doesn't know her place."

"Because she refused ceding her body before Oberon told you where to find yours?"

"That and...other things."

"Like what?" I prodded.

Faery leaned toward me. "Half of her is evil."

"Sins of the fathers, eh?"

"How could it be otherwise?" she shot back.

"Is that why you tried to feed her to the Harpies?"

Faery looked away, unwilling to answer.

I rolled my shoulders back. "Thank you for talking with me. I understand better now, but you must leave Dariyah alone. I would be devastated if something happened to her that was your doing."

"You'd find someone else."

I set my mouth in a tight line. "Really? Is that why I was alone until I met her?"

"Most of us are alone," she said, a wistful undernote in her voice. "You have me. It should be enough."

I caught sharp words before they spilled from me. Statements that would have said she hadn't been enough for Oberon. At least I was loyal to her, or trying to be.

"I am deeply appreciative for the land link. I recognize what an honor and responsibility it is," I said. "For me to be comfortable holding up my end of our arrangement, I cannot be perpetually looking over my shoulders to make sure you haven't done something to harm the woman I love."

"Why her when you could have had anybody?"

"Who knows the why of the heart?" I replied. "Dariyah is part of me. It didn't happen quickly, but one day I turned around and knew she was the only one for me." I stopped long enough to take a breath. "I was instrumental in her life too. Our bond broke through Auril's concealment spell, and freed Dariyah's wings."

"I wondered where they came from," she muttered.

"Can you give me your word?" I pressed.

"About?"

"Not harming Dariyah."

"I didn't do anything direct earlier," Faery said.

I flapped one hand. "Direct. Indirect. What I'm requesting—and it's nonnegotiable—is you will do nothing that might cause harm. Dariyah escaped Nemia by an absurdly narrow margin. She was very nearly lost in the void between worlds."

"How was I to know one of the Harpies would dart her?"

"Unless you hear otherwise, the other side—and that includes all of them—would like nothing more than Dariyah dead."

"See? We hold common ground," she smirked.

"Get over it." I was done being nice. "Immediately."

"Or?"

"I'll sever the link with you myself. I promise you won't like whoever steps into the breach my absence leaves."

"You threatened the same before."

"This isn't a threat. It's real."

"Will you hang it over my head every time I do something you don't like?"

I winced. "Nay. Dariyah is in a class by herself. Will you give me your word you'll do nothing further that might cause her to come to harm?"

Faery was silent so long, I thought she was going to dodge my request. I'd thrown down a gauntlet. If she refused to offer assurances, I'd have no choice but to sever the land link.

While I waited, I sorted through the part of me where the link resided and prepared to clip the attachment points. I'd wanted the land link for a long time before Faery offered it. Of course, it hadn't been available until Oberon let it go, but I'd prioritize Dariyah over the land link. Hell, I'd elevate her wellbeing over anything else.

When Faery began speaking, the sound of her voice was a surprise. I'd been preparing to move ahead without her. "I agree," she said, "on one condition."

"I'm listening."

"You will see this war through to its end and help me rebuild Faery no matter who wins."

I blinked a few times, digesting her request. "If the Unseelie win, they won't want me here."

"They will if I make it clear you are a part of me."

"Dariyah would be part of that package."

Faery rolled her burnished metal eyes. "If you insist, but I won't be responsible for her safety."

"So long as you don't actively sabotage her, or sell her out to our enemies, I can live with it. Do we have a deal?"

"We do," Faery replied in solemn tones and made shooing motions with both hands. "Get moving. You have a war to plan."

"And you have one to help with," I reminded her.

"I will do my job. I always do."

It wasn't a time to disagree. This discussion had gone far better than I'd anticipated it would. Knowing when to leave is half of any battle, so I withdrew. As I walked, I searched for Dariyah. She was in Auril's cottage near the Midnight Court. The door stood ajar, and I padded inside quietly. For long moments, I watched her and wished for a respite for us both. Head propped on a shoulder, she sat in a chair, sound asleep.

New lines etched into her forehead. Dark patches lay beneath both eyes, and her skin had a translucent quality. The urge to gather her into my arms and transport us both to somewhere safe was overwhelming—until I reminded myself nowhere was safe.

Not anymore. Earth might offer temporary respite, but it depended on magic too, even though mortals had no idea how fragile their existence was. Dariyah sighed in her sleep and settled deeper into the chair. I wavered between necessity and letting her sleep longer, but our desperate straits won. Waking her gently, I told her we needed to talk.

Maybe it was the needing to talk part, but her green eyes snapped open. Two vertical lines formed between her brows. "Aw geez. What happened now?"

I understood. Politics back on Earth were a bite from the same fruit, the news so universally horrible that reactions ranged from apathy to irritation to a numb indifference.

"I realize more about what's driving Faery," I told her and sketched out the bones of my conversation with the land.

Dariyah listened intently despite her distrust of Faery. When I was done, she narrowed her eyes. "I knew she didn't like me but holding Pegasus against me seems harsh. Mother was convinced Faery placed the dart."

"She might have, even though she shunted it off to one of the Harpies. She gave me her word she'd stop setting things up to create problems for you, though."

"Eh. Did you believe her?"

I nodded. "Aye, I do, mostly because she doesn't lie. She's never had cause to. She tells the truth as she sees it, and her subjects either get with the program or not. It's never been a bone of contention before."

Dariyah twisted her mouth into a scowl. "But it has. Oberon did what he wanted independent of her. Does she realize it?"

"I pointed that out, and she paid lip service to it."

Rolling her shoulders back, Dariyah got to her feet and stretched her arms over her head. Vertebrae cracked; she offered a half-baked grin. "I shouldn't sleep sitting up."

"I'm sorry my rooms in Dubrova aren't in better shape."

She shook her head. "It's okay. I've spent plenty of nights on the ground. I'm getting soft. Shouldn't we be at some kind of war strategy council? How long did I sleep, anyway?"

"Yes to the first question, and probably not long enough for the second."

The sound of raised voices reached me. Auril was arguing with someone. I couldn't make out all the words, but the discussion was heated.

Dariyah swiveled to face the door. "Crap. Did I forget to shut it? Or did you leave it standing open?"

"Does it matter?" I didn't want to add to her concerns by telling her she'd forgotten to close it.

"Nah. What the hell? That's Mother and someone having a row." She started for the door, but stopped beneath the lintel. Twisting, she looked over a shoulder. "Do you think I should intervene?"

"Probably not, but we're going to anyway. I need your mother in tiptop shape for our strategizing meeting, not worn down by a pissing contest with someone."

"She was on her way to the in-between to replenish her power," Dariyah told me. "Must have been successful because she's back. Except she could have been gone for hours. I really should have remained awake."

"You needed rest, or you wouldn't have passed out." Crossing the cottage's central room, I took her hand and we hurried toward the angry voices while I sifted through magical vibrations trying to tack down who Auril was having a spat with.

The puzzle wasn't hard to solve, and I stopped dead.

Dariyah tugged on my hand. "Come on. Why'd you stop?"

I turned her to face me. "Danu is here. It's who Auril's fighting with."

Eyes wide with surprise, Dariyah sent power of her own zinging forward. And withdrew it just as fast. "Shit. You're right. I didn't like my other grandmother much. Do you suppose this one will be a dead loss as well?"

"Ssht. She might hear you."

"Feels like the least of my problems." Dariyah jerked my hand again. "May as well do a meet-and-greet and get it over with."

I wasn't nearly as sure of the wisdom of that as she was, but neither would I leave her to face Danu by herself. We crossed the glade of the Midnight Court, and I cleared my throat. Both women had been so immersed in their heated words, neither had paid the slightest attention as we approached. Hopefully, it meant Dariyah's commentary as she speculated about this grandmother had gone unnoticed as well.

Tall and stately, Danu was wrapped in a green silk robe embroidered with black runes. Violet hair spilled down her shoulders and back almost to ground level. She and Auril were about the same height with the same broad-shouldered build; both were barefoot. A silver torc wound around Danu's throat; rings set with precious gems graced most of her fingers.

If looks had been daggers, Auril's gaze could have injured me. "Your timing is horrid," she pronounced.

The weight of Danu's gaze fell upon me, heavy with reproach. I bowed, unsure what to say, so I opted for truth. "Welcome to Faery. Thank you for your presence here because we are in desperate need of your aid."

"After unseating the balance in the magical world, now you want help?" she sneered, nostrils flaring with distain.

Humility only goes so far. "If anyone disturbed the balance," I told her, "it was Oberon, not me."

Dariyah chose that moment to step forward. "You're my other grandmother. Nice to meet you. I hope. The one on the other side of the family left a lot to be desired."

I rocked from foot to foot ready to place my body between Dariyah and Danu if the goddess decided to smite her for impertinence.

After a long pause, Danu tossed her head back and laughed. When she was done, she said, "Medusa is scarcely a hard act to follow, child."

Auril snorted. "This is the woman you were rebuking me for. She hasn't been a child for a long while. Still feeling angry?"

Danu turned to her. "You never had a sense of humor."

"When you're blaming me for all the world's ills, it's tough to maintain any kind of equanimity...Mother."

Before the conversation headed downhill again, I stepped in. "Why are you here?" I asked Danu.

"I go where I please."

I held my hands up, palms facing outward. "Of course you do. We could use all the help you have to spare, but I'm curious what drew you to Faery now. I've never seen you in Faery before."

"It does not mean I haven't been here."

I remained silent. Apologizing once was sufficient.

"She came because of Dariyah's wings," Auril said. "And the obvious link to Pegasus."

Keeping a bland expression, I absorbed the fact Danu hadn't known about Auril's long-ago decision to seduce the winged horse.

"I also came because you have reached a critical juncture, one that will set a cascade of unfortunate events into play."

"If we lose," I clarified.

"If you lose," she agreed. "Let's make certain Faery prevails."

A glance at the sky told me it was midafternoon. "We planned our next strike for the early hours of tomorrow morning," I told her.

Danu shook her head. "Too soon. We will require more time to choreograph our approach."

"Will any of the other gods be involved?" Auril asked.

"Not sure. Working on that now."

Titania bustled into our midst. "Thought I felt your presence." She bobbed her head in Danu's direction. "What are you doing here?"

"Is that any way to—?"

"Aye, 'tis," Titania cut her off. "None of my other interactions with you and yours have gone particularly well. No reason why this one should. We stand on the brink of disaster. More cooks in the kitchen aren't wise."

Auril edged toward her sister and murmured, "She means well."

"You would think that," Titania replied, not bothering to modulate her voice.

"With all due respect, my queen," I said to Titania, "we shouldn't chase Danu away."

Dariyah caught my eye before she said, "Come on, everyone, Faery's warriors are gathering at the far end of the green. We can hash out what comes next."

"What 'comes next' is what I say." Danu's fog-colored gaze landed on me.

"So long as we all agree," I said. "We have a plan sketched out. I would appreciate hearing your thoughts."

"At least someone would." Danu aimed her words at Titania, who ignored her.

Somehow, we moved as a unit toward Ysir and the others. The old librarian bolted forward and knelt before Danu. "My lady. Welcome to Faery."

The greeting echoed through the assemblage while Titania huffed disapproval. Would the adulation placate Danu, be enough for her to offer real help and not just criticism?

I took my place at the head of the group and crossed my fingers, hoping for the best. I didn't have Titania's direct experience with deities, but she'd soured on them for a reason. I wanted to draw my own conclusions, keep an open mind.

"I'll take over from here," Danu informed me. Stepping forward, she raised her arms, shouted, "Silence," and launched into a lecture about our slipshod ways.

So much for an open mind. Five minutes hadn't passed, and I already resented the goddess cataloguing our sins. Unwilling to stand by while she beat the heart out of my people, I strode purposefully to her side and said, "We would be better served planning our next offensive, my lady."

Before she told me to shut up, or turned me into a toad, I kept on talking as I described what we had planned for the wee hours of the coming morning.

CHAPTER TEN, DARIYAH

Grandmothers be damned. So far this one might be a step above Medusa, but she scarcely counted as the warm, fuzzy, cookie-baking type. One who'd welcome me into the fold. She and Mother had been arguing about me. One of the phrases I'd caught was her screaming at Mother she was a fool for birthing me.

My other take-home message was Danu hadn't known about me until very recently. It was the driving force behind her unexpected visit to Faery. Mother never talked about her own mother. I'd assumed they were estranged. I'd been spot on about that, but the bad blood between them hadn't cooled with the passing of time.

From what I'd seen so far, I didn't like Danu much better than Medusa. At least the Gorgon was unabashedly honest about what she was. Danu hid behind the skirts of civility, but beneath her "I'm a goddess" persona, she seemed just as haughty and unprincipled as Medusa. Wielding power came with a great deal of responsibility. Using it to run roughshod over those you viewed as magical inferiors was poor practice.

I was glad when Cyn put a cork in her monologue about what losers we were for getting ourselves into this mess in the first place. You'd think she'd have given Mother credit for taking one for the team by having me, but Danu appeared oblivious to the possibility any of us could be anything except a pack of failures.

I felt Mother's energy as she sidled next to me. "How'd the in-between work for you?" I asked softly.

"Very well. Thanks." Mother hesitated before asking, "Now do you see why I didn't bother mentioning her to you?"

"Or me to her, apparently." I sent a sidelong glance Mother's way.

"That too," she agreed. "I didn't want her helpful hints on childrearing. I knew all of them by heart and wasn't invested in making the same mistakes."

"That's not it," I said pointblank. "She'd have said the same things she tossed in your face earlier. If she'd known, she might have killed me before I was born."

Mother's eyes pinched at the corners, but she didn't acknowledge my speculation as accurate. Didn't matter. If I'd been off base, she'd have corrected me fast enough. Lucky me. Two grandmothers who'd rather I was dead.

Stop it, one of my inner voices instructed in sharp tones.

As usual, it was correct. Nothing I did—or didn't do—would change anyone's mind about me.

Cyn finished outlining the attack we had percolating for a few hours hence. Dragon energy bloomed all around me as they flew from journey channels and circled to land. Ash thudded down next to Cynwrigg. "You were supposed to alert me," the dragon rumbled. Smoke plumed from his nostrils.

"He's failed in his obligation to you as well, I suppose." Danu made it appear Cyn made a habit out of dereliction to duty.

Sheesh. I'd thought Faery was tough to work with. For the first time, I began to see a whole lot of plusses to my upbringing estranged from most of the magical world.

Ash lumbered in a quarter circle and stared at Danu, his eyes spinning crazily. "Did you agree to help our cause?" More steam puffed from the dragon.

"You make it appear I had a choice." Danu sniffed; her features formed a disapproving expression.

Ash folded his forelegs across his gold-scaled chest. "We discussed the advisability of including the gods."

"You have my attention, dragon, all of it."

"You're not the easiest group to work with." Ash extended a foreleg and held up a talon. "First, you rarely agree among yourselves." A second talon joined the first. "Second, you're famous for not giving your allies the whole story." He lifted another talon. "Third, you charge for your services, and the price is non-negotiable."

"Aye, and it will be steep considering we have dragon hoards to choose from," Danu said smoothly.

Cyn stepped between them, facing Danu. "Wait a minute. Before, you said you had to help because if we lose to the Gorgons and Unseelie, magic will die out. Its absence will have a trickle-down effect that would create problems for the gods."

"I did say something along those lines," Danu agreed. "So what?"

"If your ox stands to be gored too, why would you even think about charging for whatever help you provide? From my perspective, we're all in this together. Faery isn't charging you for all the work she's done holding the gates against evil."

As if she'd been waiting in the wings, listening—and she probably had been—Faery glided through a gash in the air and placed her hands on her hips. "My regent raises a valid point," she said.

Ash bugled long and loud; the dragons who'd come with him took up the cry until the Midnight Court rang with dragon song. It was eerie and beautiful and loud. When it died out, Cyn inclined his head to Ash. "Thank you for a timely prompt. This isn't a stage to dissect past failings or hurt feelings. Apologies for not letting you know about this meeting sooner. I got sidetracked, but it's not an excuse."

"Accepted," Ash said.

"Are you with us or not?" Cyn asked Danu, cutting to the meat of the problem. I was proud of him. Usually, I'm the one to ride point and throw hard questions on the table.

"Why wouldn't I be?" Danu sputtered.

"Allies work together," Cyn reminded her. "We will develop our plans with input from everyone, and then we'll stick to them as long as possible."

"What if I don't agree?" Danu's mouth was clamped into a thin bloodless line.

"We won't be able to nail down every last detail. Some of what transpires will fall into the realm of field decisions. Everyone has that latitude. It might not appear so, but I'm grateful to see you, and doubly grateful to know you and your kinsmen will be standing next to us."

"I never promised any of the other gods," she said firmly. "Your refusal to compensate us will be a sticking point."

Faery gathered her heavy hair and pushed it behind her shoulders. "Oberon still has his claws into Faery even absent the land link. He and the Unseelie King hold complementary powers. Add in the Gorgons, Harpies, Shadow Lords, and an Infernal or two, and it's quite an array of evil we face. If they overrun Faery, they will draw from my power. I won't be able to stop them."

"Their next stop after siphoning magic from Faery will be your magical reserves," Ash said to Danu. "Nothing like a taste of grandeur to make wickedness thirst for more."

Cyn whistled once; the shrill hum cut through the glade. Multiple conversations died until the only sounds were from birds flying overhead. "We must begin," he said.

"No more time to waste. Our first task is deciding if we still attack in the early hours of tomorrow morning."

I was bleary and shell-shocked. My narrow escape from Nemia, and my return trip there where we'd fought Harpies, replayed like a grade-B horror flick. My magic was mostly recovered, but my spirit—the part that had always carried me through—wasn't up to par.

I'd never had to fix that segment of things before, and I wasn't certain how to begin. Ash, Cyn, and Ysir outlined a plan I was mostly familiar with. Danu challenged it in spots, but they were relevant. She had a keen eye for ferreting out potential pitfalls.

Various mages inserted this, that, or the other concern. I should be more interested. Why wasn't I? It wasn't like me to want to retreat to a cave and yank metaphorical covers over myself. Instead of gradually pulling my head out of my ass, I was feeling worse.

Mother still stood next to me, and she hooked an arm with mine. "What's wrong?" she asked softly.

"Not sure," I whispered back, "but I feel like crap."

Familiar magic jabbed me, moving from spot to spot—the mage equivalent of a physical exam. Mother had done this to me so many times, I'd learned to sit still and tolerate her less-than-gentle probing.

"Mmph," she mumbled.

"What's that supposed to mean?" I switched to mind speech, mostly so we wouldn't interrupt anyone else's concentration.

Rather than answering, the varied scents of her power

—lupine, lemon, and brandy—enveloped me. When they cleared, we were in her cottage. "We shouldn't have left," I protested.

"Not much choice." Mother's tone was brisk, all business. "Take off your top."

"Why? Tell me what you think is wrong with me."

"Harpy poisoning. I need to see your back and chest."

I quit arguing. I'd dug a Harpy's dart out of my magical center. Had I broken it? Missed some tiny bit that was still working its mayhem inside me? After shrugging out of my jacket, I pushed my button-down top over my shoulders. None of my pullover tops worked anymore. My wings got in the way. A quick glance at my breasts sent breath whooshing from me.

They were mottled with black splotches and reddish lines. My wings spread of their own accord, knocking into Mother who was walking around me in a circle still probing. She repositioned herself so she faced me and looked me dead in the eyes. "This isn't good."

"What isn't good? Christ, Mother. This is not a time for your seer riddles." A wave of dizziness threatened to unbalance me. I gripped a nearby chair so I wouldn't fall over.

"Lie down," she said. "I'll do what I can, but it won't be pleasant."

My teeth had begun to chatter. I clamped my jaws together and pushed words out with effort. "Tell me exactly what's wrong and what you plan to do about it."

"We don't have much time—" she began.

"I refuse to believe two minutes will make much difference."

"Compromise?" Usually when she said that she was smiling, but not now. It told me how grave my situation was.

"What?"

"Lie down, let me begin, and I'll tell you what I think happened."

Vertigo made the room spin crazily. It was lie down or fall down. I chose the former and staggered to the bed. Separated from the rest of the cottage by a curtain, it was a simple, narrow affair. One of my wings crushed as I fell on it. Grunting with effort, I moved to accommodate its small bones and feathers.

Mother constructed a healing tent. I'd given up and shut my eyes, but I felt its folds settle over me. "Harpies subdue their victims in two ways," Mother said as a red-hot tide of power scorched my feet and ankles before edging upward.

It took all my willpower not to shriek at the agony burning every nerve ending to a cinder.

"They capture you directly by forcing you to look at them," she went on, "and then they suck your soul out through your mouth. The second method involves placing something inside a victim that will eventually render them unconscious. The bit of dark power has a communication function that alerts whichever Harpy set the trap when her victim is ripe for the plucking."

"And then the soul-sucking commences. But I got the

dart out." My words were so slurred, I almost couldn't recognize them.

"Apparently, not all of it, but you have the general picture. Right now, toxins are pumping through your body. If we'd caught this earlier…"

I started to protest I hadn't felt all that bad until maybe an hour ago, but it was too difficult to get my mouth to cooperate.

"What are you doing here?" a shrill voice demanded. Confusion reigned until I recognized someone had come to Mother's house. I tried to crack an eyelid to see who it was, but much like speech, eyelid cracking was beyond me.

"Mother. For once in your life do something besides criticizing me," my own mother said. At least it clarified who was here.

"Aye, but you never should have left… Awk. Looks like Harpy poisoning. Why didn't you say something?"

"Because you never gave me a chance," Mother replied sourly.

Danu stood over me. I felt her power as she poked and prodded, and I bit hard on my lip so I wouldn't cry out. I'd be damned if I'd give her the satisfaction of hearing me yelp.

"Knock her out," Danu instructed. "Otherwise this will be beyond her ability to tolerate."

"Want to be awake," I slurred, my control freak genes shooting to the fore. While I trusted Mother, I did not trust Danu. At all.

"Too bad," the goddess told me.

Darkness descended. I fought with everything I had, clung to departing consciousness like a drowning man clinging to a spar. It didn't buy me shit. Before the last of my sentience fled, the pain scouring me ratcheted upward by a factor of a hundred. After a brief skirmish between my fear and the pain, agony won out, and I plummeted downward.

I fell for a long time through a Halloween house of horrors. As I plunged downward, I skirted an eerie awareness where I wasn't exactly awake. Neither was I deeply enough asleep to ignore everything around me. Creepy misshapen forms with long nails and skeletal fingers grabbed at me. Bony protuberances ripped chunks of my flesh, and I kept right on falling. My wings shredded, only to grow and shred again. Pain was a constant companion. Turning in my passageway, I puked until my stomach was empty. But I still had dry heaves.

Screams roared out of me until my throat was swollen and raw. I wanted Cyn, but he was busy. Faery needed him. My puny problems could wait. Finally, after forever—a forever punctuated by torture beyond my worst imaginings, except somehow I was still breathing—I curled into a ball and waited for death.

Part of me didn't want to give up, but a much bigger part was done. I couldn't fight anymore. The only thing I wanted was for the pain to go away and leave me be. Hot. Cold. Knives. Explosions that left me raw and bleeding. I couldn't catch a break no matter what I did. Whether I ended up in the *Dreaming*—or in Hell—didn't matter. So long as the agony bleaching my bones to dust went away.

Tears came until there were no more.

This would be a fine time for my astral self to separate from my pain-racked body, but it remained stubbornly attached.

Lupine and lemon teased my nostrils. I shook my head to dispel the hallucination. I was dead, or not far from it. Mother was very much alive. Someone had to fight off the Unseelie, and I was out of the picture.

A familiar hand closed around my arm. I yelped. Hmmm. Not dead after all. This time when I struggled to open my eyes, I managed to crack one of them. Mother leaned over me, her long hair falling in my face.

"Sit up, Dariyah. You'll get past this."

"Let's give credit where it's due." Danu's dry voice held a satisfied note. "I cleared the poison, but it was an uphill battle. Why on earth didn't you say something sooner?" She stuck her face next to mine.

"Because I had no idea." I choked on the words, the sour taste of vomit thick in my mouth. "Water."

"It's not as if she's run into this before," Mother said, rising to my defense as she handed me a carafe.

I tried to hold it, but my fingers wouldn't cooperate, so she tipped swallows into my mouth. "Still feel like shit," I mumbled.

"It will pass," Danu said. "Sit up like your mother told you. I have some repair work to do on those wings."

Now wasn't a time to remind her the wings were a

product of the "bad" side of my genetics. They hurt, but so did all the rest of me. "What did you two do?" I croaked.

"Stripped away everything and started over," Danu said.

I felt her moving the small bones in my wings this way and that. Some must have broken because more pain buffeted me. Comparatively, this discomfort was mild. I felt Cyn's energy before I saw him.

He skidded into the cottage and came to a halt next to the bed. The small sleeping area had been crowded with three of us, and now we bumped into one another. "What happened?" he thundered.

"She will recover," Mother said.

"She looks like a train ran over her. What happened?" he repeated and fell to his knees, taking my hands in his.

"Harpy poison. At least we know who placed the dart," I managed. My throat was still raw, and my lips chapped with deeply cut places.

"Damn my eyes." Cyn shook his head. "How'd you figure it out?"

"I almost didn't," Mother replied. "If I hadn't been standing next to her when the poison really took off, we'd have had a different outcome."

"I'm who set this right," Danu said.

"Thank you," I croaked. "Very much."

"Aye, you have my undying thanks as well," Cyn told the goddess. She was still working on my wings, but they were feeling more like they'd function again.

"What happened after we left?" Auril asked him.

"We moved everything forward by a day," he answered. "To give Danu time to recruit a few more of her own."

"Wise," the goddess muttered and stepped from behind the bed. "Keep those quiet for a couple of hours. They'll mend, along with the rest of you."

I managed to grip the container with water and took a few more swallows. "Thank you so much."

"You already thanked me, child. If we didn't share blood, I would have had a much more difficult time."

"That will be one dead Harpy," Cyn growled.

"Eh, kill them all. They outlived whatever usefulness they had a few hundred years ago," Danu said.

"Is she all right?" Ash called from outside the cottage.

"She will be," Cyn told him.

A staunch bugle told me how relieved he was by my recovery. I was too, now that it had sunk in I wasn't going to die. I'd given up, something I wasn't proud of, but no one had to know it except me.

"Can I move her?" Cyn asked Mother and Danu.

"Where?" the goddess asked.

"She needs rest and food," Cynwrigg replied. "It's simpler for me to provide both on Earth."

"I thought you were going after the Harpy," Danu arched golden brows.

"I am, but Dariyah's needs come first. Besides, I'll see the Harpies soon enough. They'll be at the next skirmish."

"Are you ever going to tell her what her name is?" Danu directed her words at Mother.

"When the time is right." Mother sounded tired. She must have been frantic she'd lose me forever.

All those months when I'd have given my right hand to know my name marched through my head. Perspective followed. "I'm not in a hurry," I told my kinswomen.

"What changed?" Mother asked.

I shrugged and struggled to sit, dangling my legs off the edge of the bed. "I'm not sure. Not knowing my true name was a blessing when Pegasus tried to drag it from me. I'm going to trust it will show up when I need it most, not when I'm merely curious and feeling marginalized."

"Are you well enough for me to take us to your flat?" Cyn asked.

I pushed off the bed and took a few unsteady steps. Because I didn't fall on my face, I walked outside. Ash scooped me into his forelegs and held me against his chest. I felt the thrum of his heart as he poured dragon magic into me. By the time he set me down, everyone else stood outside too.

I moved to Cyn's side. "Yes, I'm well enough to leave." While he cobbled a spell together, I walked to Danu and held out a hand.

She ignored it and wrapped her arms around me while she spoke into my mind. *"I misjudged you, child. You have spirit, and a great deal of inner strength."*

"If you'd been right the first time," I retorted, *"and I'd been weak as yesterday's tea, would you have bothered to salvage me?"*

She tightened her hold on me before letting go. "If I'd

known how entertaining you were, I'd have gotten to know you sooner."

"Except you didn't realize I existed."

She lifted her broad shoulders in a small shrug. "I would have figured it out eventually. After all, you carry my blood."

Returning to Cyn's side, I leaned into him as his magic wrapped me in a soothing cloak. "Food or sleep?" he asked.

"Both, but maybe sleep first."

"We'll go to your flat. I can grab takeout from one of the places down the street. Do you want to talk about what happened?"

"Yeah. Nope. Aw crap, I don't know. Guess I missed some of the Harpy's dart, and it took a while to manifest its death chant."

The worried expression on his face shaded to half a smile. "You'll be yourself in no time. You're joking about this."

"Maybe so, but if I don't lighten the mood, I'll be depressed as fuck I missed something that was nearly the end of me."

"Want to know what I think happened?"

"Sure."

He nodded. "I bet there were two darts. You removed the critical one, and it allowed your teleport spell to finish its trajectory and drop you at Fire Mountain."

I finished his thought for him. "And I was so relieved, it never occurred to me to search for another."

"Harpies are nothing if not thorough. It's something we should keep in mind."

The next part was quick. From Cyn's arms to my flat to my cat nestled against me. Taking care not to crush my healing wings, I lay on my stomach and relaxed so sleep could finish healing me. No wonder I'd passed out in Mother's cottage earlier. The poison had been at work even then.

I'd been lucky. Or maybe luck hadn't had anything to do with it. I had a role to play, one that was still developing. As I tried to tease out the particulars, my weary brain checked out.

CHAPTER ELEVEN, CYN

I had food ready each time Dariyah awakened. First we ate Chinese. Then Italian. The cat had a heyday polishing what was left in the takeout containers. I dozed off and on. Mostly, I watched over Dariyah. I hadn't realized she and Auril were gone until I felt her desperation and anguish through our link. It brought me on a dead run, but I'd missed the main event.

At least Danu had warmed to her granddaughter. It was a major improvement from her earlier shouting match with Auril where she'd catalogued all the ways she'd been a disappointment. Out of all of us, Titania had the most up-close-and-personal experience with the gods. Her advice had been to steer well clear, and I was beginning to understand her reasoning.

Despite Danu and her kin being wild cards, I was relieved they'd shore up our efforts. Maybe we could get by with one more battle rather than the two Auril had prophesied. I was sick to my bones of war and strife and watching friends die. I'd said it before, but if Oberon ever crossed my path again, I'd finish him myself.

No sending him to Faery where he'd sweettalk his way to freedom. Or anywhere else. No *Dreaming* for him, either. He hadn't earned the privilege. If the only thing he'd done was abandoning Faery, I'd have gladly consigned him to a cushy afterlife. But he hadn't quit there. Not by a longshot.

Dariyah sighed in her sleep and rolled over. I figured the positional shift was safe enough because her wings had healed. I'd been checking them—and the rest of her too—at intervals. If she'd taken a turn for the worse, I'd have hustled her back to Faery. Her magic felt different to me, the change significant. Danu had left a trail a kilometer wide, marking Dariyah as one of her own. Ash had pumped her chock-full of dragon essence. What with it all, I could scarcely sense Pegasus, only finding traces because I knew what to look for.

Danu must have grabbed the opportunity to replace what she perceived as evil with her own brand of enchantment. Because Dariyah already had her blood, the net effect strengthened her power. I nodded to myself. We needed every bit of capacity at our disposal. The Unseelie king had to be as fed up with warfare as I was. While more patient than Oberon, he still preferred leisure to the never-ending blood and grit of war.

Magical wars never lasted long, so it baffled me this one

had developed a life all its own. The last lengthy war had been when the dragons imprisoned the Shadow Lords—and it had been over far quicker than this one.

I was considering where to go for more takeout when Dariyah turned in my arms and wrapped hers around me. "How long was I out?"

"A while. Do you remember eating?"

She shook her head against my shoulder. "Not really, but at least I feel like myself again. It's a massive relief. Back in Faery I felt depressed, despondent. It cued me something was off when I didn't give fuck all about anything. Things went downhill so fast once they got rolling, I didn't have much opportunity to analyze the problem."

"Thank all the gods your mother was nearby. I should have felt something, but by the time I picked up there was anything amiss..." Guilt jabbed me. I vowed to never let my attention stray so far again.

"You can't blame yourself."

I did, but we had to move forward. Perseverating on the past never accomplished much of anything.

She exhaled gently. "We should get back to Faery, but I don't want to move. Not quite yet."

"We have time. Not a lot, but some." I threaded my fingers into her tangled hair and held her head against me. Midnight purred louder, which was saying something. He'd been tucked against Dariyah ever since we arrived.

"Enough to clean up?"

Suddenly, a shower sounded like a wonderful idea. Both

of us stank of blood and guts and fire residue. I didn't have clean clothes here, but my own place was close enough to grab something and return. I kissed her forehead and both cheeks. "Don't use all the hot water. I'll be back with something else to wear."

"It's the same thing you did a while back," she teased. "Do you have maid service at your house to make sure you don't run out of clean clothes?"

I chuckled. "As a matter of fact, I do. A local laundry picks up and delivers."

"Ha." She crinkled her nose at me. "I knew it. Do you suppose they'd wash a few things of mine?"

"You're serious." It surprised me.

"Yeah. Of course, I'm serious. When do you think I'll find time to even locate where the laundromat is in this complex? My old flat had a washer and dryer. This one doesn't. I'm low on fresh clothes, so it's either wash what I have or buy more."

I hated to disentangle my limbs from hers, but we'd stolen more than our share of break time. "Make me up a sack of laundry. I'll add it to mine. Should give the service something to gossip about."

Dariyah rolled first to a sit and then to her feet. Midnight yowled in protest, but he padded to his kibble dish and began munching as a consolation activity. After rooting in one of the kitchen cabinets, Dariyah came up with a large plastic garbage sack. A quick transit of the room added pants, socks, tops, and underwear to the bag. Next, she bent to unlace her boots and toe them off. She shrugged out of her top and pants until she was down to a pair of black lace panties.

The sight of her sans clothing was incredible. She was alluring, seductive, and a knockout without any effort at all on her part to do anything but be herself. My throat thickened, and my words held a raspy edge when I said, "You're not making this easy."

Pressure built south of my waistline as my cock thickened to a pillar against my belly.

She folded her wings forward so they hid most of her breasts and torso. "Is that better?" With an enigmatic smile worthy of the Mona Lisa, she stripped off her panties, stuffed them in the bag along with everything else, and handed it to me. "See you in the shower."

I stared after her as she turned and loped toward the bathroom before reminding myself I had a task that needed attention. After the quickest teleport spells on record, I was back in her living room, fresh garments hung over one arm and my cock still wildly erect. Somehow my inflated condition had survived the trip to my place and back. I'd even put a rush on the latest laundry order. It should be back by tomorrow.

Goddess only knew where we'd be then, but at least we'd have fresh clothes waiting for us when we got back here. The sound of running water beckoned. I draped my assorted clean clothing over the kitchen counter before finding my way to the steamy bathroom, shedding garments as I went, with my shoes and trousers the last to go.

Sliding the glass shower door open, I stepped over the low wall of the tub. A dripping Dariyah turned away from the spray and hugged me close. Her wet, soapy skin was slippery and arousing.

"That was quick," she teased. "Couldn't stay away, huh?"

"With you naked in the shower? You must be joking." I closed my arms around her and laced my fingers into her wings. Nowhere near as wet as the rest of her, they seemed to have some innate mechanism to not absorb water.

Her nipples pebbled against my chest. Overcome with blind need, I bent my head and kissed her, mouth crashing down on hers. Nothing elegant about what came next. Driven by lust and the knowledge I'd nearly lost her, our kiss turned savage as we bit, licked blood, and bit some more. Our tongues tangled; our teeth clanked together. The heat from our bodies and panting breath added to the steam filling the tiny enclosure.

I kneaded the globes of her high tight ass; she raked her nails down my back. The water was turning cold, but I barely noticed as I turned her away from me and seated myself at the entrance to her body. Reaching around, I took a breast in each hand, twirling and pinching the nipples. Her hips bucked toward me, and I pushed inside the slick fire of her body.

I tried for slow, and might have managed it for the first stroke or two. Her muscles snugged around me until my cock was fully encased. I stayed quiet within her, savoring the cascade of sensation. With a light fluttery motion, she tightened around me, I twitched back before withdrawing until only the head of my cock lay within her folds. One of my hands found its way from a breast to her swollen nub, and I teased it in a circular pattern.

Hands settled on my ass; she'd reached around me to pull me back inside. The next strokes were faster. I drummed my fingers on her clit and fucked her from behind. My heart thumped double-time in my chest. Every nerve came alive with the magic she and I wove together. The rest of the world fell away until she and I were all that mattered. The places our bodies connected, the places our hearts and souls intertwined glowed with an inner brilliance. Motes of magic swirled around us, heightening our pleasure.

When the first spasms of her orgasm fluttered around me, I added magic to enhance her release, and still more magic so she'd keep on coming. After the third wave crested, I let myself go as I marked her, claimed her, strengthened our bond to each other.

The sensation roaring through me, and my thoughts about marking and claiming were far removed from the world we lived in, the Earth one. They were part of Faery, though. Of a long, storied tradition I was far closer to understanding than I'd ever been before.

"Mmmm." Dariyah leaned into me, panting and purring at the same time.

"Mmmm, back at ya," I murmured and directed a bit of magic to warm the water back up. "Did you notice we've been standing under a stone-cold spray?"

"Did you?" She climbed off my cock and turned until she faced me.

I shook my head. "The only thing I noticed was you."

"That was the right answer." She kissed me quick and deep before letting go. "You need to clean up, and then we're leaving."

"There's my little taskmistress. For a while I was wondering what you'd done with her." We traded places, and I grabbed a bottle of liquid soap, the kind that's all things to all people. Shampoo, body wash, you name it.

"Mother would be proud of me. For staying on task." Dariyah laughed and stepped out of the shower.

By the time I was done, maybe all of five minutes, she'd left the bathroom. I dried myself and tripped over the pile of shoes and pants I'd left next to the bathroom door. I'd need the shoes, so I sorted them and went to hunt for the garments I'd left in the kitchen.

Dariyah was dressed and braiding her hair out of the way. It was a good idea, so I did the same. Not braids, but I gathered my heavy locks into a horse's tail and secured it with a bit of leather low on my neck. Midnight was curled up between his food dishes. Dariyah must have refilled them.

I'd felt the weight of her gaze as I pulled clothes on. "You're so pretty," she said. "I could look at you forever."

"What if I feel the same?"

"Narcissus?"

I laughed. "Not even. The same but reversed. I'd rather look at you than do almost anything else."

"Almost?" She arched a russet brow.

I walked close and swatted her ass. "Hussy. But one with the finest ass in all the worlds. On a more serious note, something came to me after our tryst in the shower."

She cast a pointed look my way. "What might that be? Wives you've stashed elsewhere? If there are, I'll make short work of them."

"Nothing that sinister, I'm afraid. If you need a bad boy in your life, I'm not him."

"I was joking. Pretty soon there won't be any more jokes. We'll be in the midst of the next battle. Gah. I hope the dragons get along with the gods. Sometimes when there are too many cooks, the kitchen catches fire."

I reached for one of her hands, and she laced her fingers with mine. "What an apt analogy, given our dragon allies."

Her eyes developed a soft mistiness. "I'll be serious. What did you want to tell me?"

"It was more of a clarification, an understanding of what our joining truly means. What came to me was you're my destiny, but I'm yours too. Unless I'm mistaken, and I don't believe I am, we're the next king and queen of Faery. It's why the mate bond is in play."

Her eyes widened. "Why would you believe that? You might have royal blood, but I'm mostly a bastard spawn."

"Oh? Think about it."

Her brow furrowed. "Erm, when you put it that way, I suppose some of that bastard blood is royal."

"Try all of it," I suggested.

"I'm not used to thinking of Mother as the queen of air and darkness. To me, she's always been just Mother."

"How about Danu?" I inquired archly. "You've got a goddess connection too. She did a bit of rearranging while she healed you."

"What kind of rearranging? I've been either too trashed to check—or otherwise occupied."

"Otherwise occupied? Is that what we're calling it now?" I teased.

"You didn't answer me." She squeezed my hand tighter.

"There's a lot more of Danu in your magic now. I had to look deep to find anything of Pegasus." I blew out a breath before continuing. "In truth, if I hadn't known about the winged horse, I'd be hard pressed to locate him anywhere in you."

Dariyah narrowed her eyes. "Fascinating. Wonder what the hell she did. I wasn't aware magic could manipulate genetics."

"You can ask, but I don't expect she'll tell you."

"Probably not." Dariyah licked her lower lip. "I've had a bunch of add-ons lately. Don't forget the dragons."

"Something bigger than us is propelling us forward," I explained, surer than ever I was onto something. "None of this happened by accident, starting with you accepting Oberon's job posting to spy on me."

"Didn't feel that way at the time," she murmured. "If I'd been aware I was falling headlong into my, uh, destiny, I'd have run the other way."

"You wouldn't have been able to."

"You sound certain about it," she said.

"Because I am. Are you ready to leave?" At her nod, I went on. "We should grab something to eat. Who knows what we'll find at the other end of the next journey spell. We can eat on the way and bring whatever's left back to Faery."

"Remind me. What did I have when I was too wiped out to recall eating anything."

"Crap Chinese and even crappier Italian."

She snorted. "Not a fan of fast food, huh?"

"Nope. How can you be?" I asked her, adding, "You must remember when food was carefully prepared by people who actually gave a shit about how it turned out."

Dariyah nodded thoughtfully. "Yeah. I also remember botulism, e-coli poisoning, and a bunch of other illnesses that were linked to that lovingly prepared fare." She shrugged. "Every era has plusses. And minuses."

I'd released her hand a while ago. "You didn't say much about my king and queen of Faery theory."

The smile that had accompanied our earlier banter faded. "I'm still thinking about it. You deserve to be Faery's king. It's a logical step up from regent."

She stopped there, so I tossed out, "But you don't deserve to be Faery's queen?"

Twin vertical lines formed between her eyebrows. "Maybe deserve isn't quite right. I don't feel worthy of such an august position in a place I barely know. And where the people don't know me, either."

I didn't do any cheerleading. Spouting platitudes about

everyone loving her once they got to know her wouldn't be helpful. She'd begun to consider the possibility, and it was enough for now.

Dariyah ruffled Midnight's matted fur and then walked toward the door. I followed her out; we trotted down metal risers to street level. Starbucks was less than a block down on the corner. A few minutes later, sacks and cups in hand, we faded into the same alley we'd used last time we'd refueled from the coffee shop chain. It hadn't been all that long ago, but it seemed like it.

I kindled a journey spell and took a sip of my Americano. It was hot, bitter, and strong enough to stand a spoon. Just how I liked it. "I'm getting ahead of things," I said, "but after we win, I want to make some changes in Faery."

"We have to win, first," she reminded me around a mouthful of ham-and-egg croissant.

"Certainly, goes without saying, but I want Faery to be more of a land ruled by its people. I never cared for Oberon's top-down structure."

"Would you disband the court?" Dariyah washed down food with her coffee.

"Not disband, but I'd change it to a venue anyone could access." I unwrapped my own sandwich, a turkey-pita affair, and took a bite. One thing I'll say for Starbucks, they're consistent. The same sandwich tasted the same no matter which shop it originated from. I suspected they had central kitchens and a distribution network, but I'd never cared enough to chase it down.

"No more court of the fallen?"

"Gods, I hope not." We popped out at the bottom of the steps leading to the casino and started walking toward the Midnight Court. I shook my head to clear my thoughts. I was looking ahead—and assuming victory—because the alternative was too painful to bear.

"You've given this a lot of thought."

I shrugged. "Not a lot, but some. I want to add more delegates, mages and animals who represent everyone living in Faery. But anyone can visit the court anytime they need something. The delegates would become more problem-solvers than edict-creators."

"I thought Oberon fashioned all the edicts," Dariyah said, "and expected the court to carry them out."

It was true. He'd expected unwavering compliance and been quick to cast blame when something didn't work as he'd wished it to. My skin tingled as we crossed the barrier between Earth and Faery. I moved in front of Dariyah and hugged her, careful of her lunch sack and coffee and wings.

"I love you. Promise you'll be careful."

She muffled a snort. "How about if you do the same?"

"It's not me they're after."

Her expression grew serious. "I'll do the best I can. After all, I want to be part of the next installment as you figure out what the court of destiny looks like."

I grinned. "Catchy. I like it way better than Titania's court of the fallen."

"Yeah. Me too."

I'd been listening carefully, expecting the ring of a

battle in progress to batter my ears. It didn't. "Everything seems quiet," I ventured.

"Seems is one thing. Let's make certain it's not an illusion."

Together, we hustled forward. Breath swooshed from me as I caught sight of friends in small groups chatting quietly. I'd felt torn about leaving Faery, but Dariyah had recovered faster away from the war-torn landscape and her mother and grandmother hovering as they bickered.

"Finally." Auril raced toward us.

"We came as soon as I was better," Dariyah told her mother.

"I was just preparing to look for you."

I wiped my mind clear of steamy memories of our love-making and hoped I'd been quick enough. I could just envision Auril stomping into the bathroom and ordering us to leave off.

Before she could launch into a lecture about how we'd been gone too long, I said, "What transpired during our absence? Leave nothing out."

Auril nailed me with an incredulous look, one that said she did not answer to me, period. I expected her to follow the look with words, and she did, but they were the ones I'd requested.

We crossed the glade, and she filled me in on the hours we'd been gone. I sensed how close she'd been to blowing me off. Apparently, she'd decided we needed a chain of command if we were going to survive the next onslaught.

❧ 12 ❧

CHAPTER TWELVE, DARIYAH

Mother was surprisingly compliant. I didn't understand why, but I was grateful she hadn't told Cyn to pound sand and left in a huff. Leaving would have meant walking away from me too, and she wasn't willing to do that. Not right now. Probably I was still riding the la-la cushion of her relief I hadn't succumbed to Harpy toxin.

Turned out we hadn't missed much. We'd been gone for nearly twelve hours. During that time, Faery's troops had firmed up their composition. I was still assigned to the crew I'd led last time. The dragons were due back soon, and Danu had gone in search of a few other gods who might be willing to help out.

No one had checked on Dubrova or the Unseelie camp. And no one had seen Faery. The latter wasn't unexpected. She wasn't inclined to hang out with anyone. I'd finished my sandwich and pastry and slugged back the remnants of my coffee. If I ended up living in Faery, I'd have to bring beans in by the sack. Tea was fine and well, but there was nothing like a hot, bitter cup of freshly ground coffee to hit the spot.

My thoughts brought me up short. Was I actually contemplating living here? Up until a few hours ago, I'd considered myself a visitor. I hadn't exactly worked out how Cyn and I would manage our brand-new status as a couple, but my assumption had been we'd spend most of our time on Earth.

It was a logical go-to place for me; I'd lived there since leaving Mother's world. Despite mortals being a substantial pain in the arse, I'd become fond of Earth, and—

"I'm going to look in on Dubrova." Cyn nudged me. "Want to ride along?"

I crumpled up my Starbuck's bags and added Cyn's before vaporizing our trash with a bit of magic. From what I'd seen, paper products hadn't made it to Faery. Trash wasn't an issue here, and I didn't want to make it one.

"Sure. I'll come," I told him. "Faery knows we're back, right?"

Cyn shrugged. "I'm sure she does, but I haven't talked with her. We should do that too, so long as we're out and about."

"You make it sound like a field trip," I murmured.

"More like a reconnaissance." A corner of his mouth twisted downward. "That's a field trip on steroids."

"Cute." I mock swatted him, glad he had a sense of

humor. Most men take themselves far too seriously. Mother hadn't said anything after she finished her rundown on what we'd missed. She curled her fingers around my lower arm and said, "Wait a moment. I want to check on something."

My skin prickled as she did her usual poke-and-prod routine. "I really am all right," I said and tried to duck from beneath her examination without success.

She jabbed me in the same spot three times in a row. It was in the region of my solar plexus, and when she worked me over, it felt sore. Her brows were knitted into a thin line; it was her worried look.

"What are you looking for?" Cyn asked.

Mother didn't answer, but she did let go of me. "Seems all right," she muttered.

Crap. Here we go again. "What seems all right?" I asked, my tone pointed.

"There's a junction point, one where different magics cross over—" she began.

"Plain language, please," I cut in.

Mother nodded. "Danu made...alterations. I wanted to make certain she didn't leave anything behind, like a mechanism to track your whereabouts. Or something subtle where she'd be able to manipulate your thoughts and actions."

"No matter how subtle it was, I'd know about it," I protested.

Mother shook her head. "Nay. You wouldn't. I spent a century picking out the clever threads she'd woven into my magic. Some had spent so long within me, they were indistinguishable from my own talents."

"She did leave magic within Dariyah," Cyn noted.

"Aye, but what she fashioned were obvious replacements for Pegasus's portions. Nothing underhanded that I could glean, and I've become adept at teasing out her handiwork."

"Was that what the two of you argued over?" I asked.

Mother nodded. "One of the things. I was sick of her controlling me." She scrunched her eyes to slits. "It was never as if she was the kind of mother who stood by on a day-to-day basis. She'd show up on her own schedule, issue orders, and vanish again."

"Who took care of you?" Cyn asked.

Mother's mouth split into a wry smile. "You'd be surprised how little care magical children require. I was on my own from the time I was three or four. Before that, faeries and nymphs made sure I had what I required."

I wanted to know so many things. Like whom her father had been, and why he hadn't been there, but none of those things were important. Nor would they make a difference in the upcoming battle. Contrary to Mother's assertion, I'd have known if something was amiss with my magic. Ignoring the odd depression prior to my collapse had been stupid.

I might make mistakes, but at least I didn't generally repeat them.

"We should leave," I told Cyn and gathered power into a spell.

"I'll be gone for a short while too," Mother told us. Before I could ask where, she added, "I'm going to stop by Fire Mountain and run a few things past the seers. My last couple of scrying episodes have yielded positive news, but I want to check my impressions against theirs before I say anything."

"How long will the world where we lived screw up your visions?" I asked, not bothering to mention her usual accounts detailing what she'd discovered were so vague as to be meaningless.

"Wish I knew the answer to that," she replied. "I don't. But when what I come up with matches other seers' impressions several times running, I'll begin to trust my foreseeing is true again. Replenishing my power from the in-between is helping."

"Because it's a neutral source," Cyn said.

Mother nodded. "Aye, not one tainted by goddess only knows what. A false sense of importance, perhaps, when she inserted her own twists here and there in an attempt to interact with me."

I extended my casting to include Cyn and swept us to our usual vantage point behind the ruins of Dubrova. My spell was clearing, and I blinked a few times certain my eyes were playing tricks. "What in the hell is all that?" I mumbled.

"Part of the castle appears to be rebuilding itself, well beyond the west wing Oberon was putting back together," Cyn said softly. "I'm not sure how or who's behind it."

"That last bit, the 'who,' is critical," I agreed and edged

nearer, reaching out with strands of seeking power to gather information. Unseelie energy bombarded me from every side but behind. They hadn't left—fat chance. Neither had their numbers decreased below what was left once Ysir and Mother wiped out the cloned versions.

The *clank* of rocks against wood drew my gaze to a turret that seemed to be repairing itself. As I watched, two full rows of stones clunked into place followed by three more. At this rate, the tower would be whole within the hour.

Cyn's magic shrouded me, replete with his usual whiskey-and-wildflower scents. I tested the ward to make sure it concealed us before we moved out of the castle's broad shadow to a vantage point atop a small knoll. Sure enough, Unseelie tents stretched as far as I could see, wrapping around the castle both inside and outside its gates.

I didn't really want to take the time to dissect what was going on with the turret, but I couldn't afford not to. No one on the ground was paying it the slightest heed, which suggested they knew about the reconstruction and were all in favor of rebuilding the castle, no doubt so they could move right in.

Cyn and I edged around the perimeter of the camp. We remained absolutely silent. No mind speech, either. Mages could detect anything magical like hunting dogs ferreted out game for their gun-toting masters. Back at our starting point, we skirted the moat and hurried to the rear of Dubrova. Sure enough, the turret was only a few layers from complete. Mortar materialized, slapping itself between the stones.

It was so bizarre, I switched to my psychic view, expecting to see a horde of invisible workmen with trowels. No such luck. The mortar originated in tubs on the ground. Those were manned by Unseelie who chucked big globs at the stones to stabilize them. But they were only managing the mortar part. The stones were bouncing upward of their own volition from the rubble pile that had once been Dubrova Castle.

Cyn angled a sharp look my way and gestured for me to follow him. Since we shared a ward, I wouldn't have done anything else. Not being able to talk was an impediment. We hurried north until we'd put distance between ourselves and the castle's bulk.

"This is far enough away," Cyn said and dismantled his ward.

Something about the set of his shoulders alerted me things might be worse than I thought. "What was that back there?" I asked.

"Faery is helping rebuild the castle."

I fell back a pace, mouth hanging open before I snapped it shut. "What? How can you be certain? I felt around and didn't sense her at all."

"You don't hold the land link," he said, sounding weary.

I didn't blame him. If he was right, we were screwed. Maybe not totally, but we'd be fighting the land along with the Unseelie. "I don't get it," I growled. "Why would she help them? Especially when she does so little to aid us."

"She told me at one point she didn't care about rebuilding Dubrova," Cyn reminded me. "She's our next stop. And I'm not leaving until she spits out answers." The air around him took on a glow as he summoned power.

I shook my head. "We should walk, not teleport. What if a bunch of Unseelie are in that cave of hers? Or worse, Shadow Lords or Oberon."

"Gotcha." He took off at a lope with me next to him.

After a few minutes he slowed, clearly hunting for something before ducking through a break in a rocky wall. The cave within led to a series of tunnels winding downward.

"How many of these entrances are there?" I asked.

"Lots. It's one of the ways I entertained myself as a lad. Hunting for them. The other Fae used to tease me about having dwarf blood." After two more loops of corridor, he glanced my way, put a finger over his lips, and dialed back the illumination from his mage light until it was the barest glow.

I doused mine and redirected magic to keep from tripping or sloughing sideways into the many potholes dotting our path. At intervals, I directed a quick beam of seeking magic, but I never detected anything down here except us.

Not even Faery.

We rounded a corner, and everything looked familiar. We'd rejoined the route I knew, and the crystal cave was only about a hundred paces ahead. No voices. No magic that shouldn't be here. At least, not on the surface. Like us, other mages could be covered in spells.

Faery's cave was empty. Cyn dialed back his warding and brightened his light. He started at the far end of the rounded enclosure and shone his light on the rocky floor and crystal-studded walls, bending to run his fingertips over a few spots. The crystals were beautiful, but today I wasn't paying their iridescent glory any heed.

"What are you looking for?" I asked, fully intending to help.

"Clues. Anything. My link to the land has been quiescent. It's still intact, but I cannot reach her."

"Big surprise. She's probably ashamed."

He shook his head and straightened, facing me. "Shame isn't part of her makeup. I'm wondering if she wasn't taken against her will and is being forced to cooperate."

I angled my head to one side. It wasn't a place my thoughts would have gone, but then Faery hadn't exactly made my favorite-person list. "Who could subjugate her?"

"Not sure. Probably the Gorgons would be sufficient without assistance from Infernals or Harpies or Shadow Lords. Remember how she skedaddled out of your body after Medusa nabbed you?"

"Not likely to forget that one," I snarked.

"You're still pissed. I get it, but for the moment could you lay it aside?" Cyn gripped my arm.

"Yeah. I can do that. You're worried about her."

"Damn straight, I am. She rarely greets me—or says goodbye—but neither does much time pass when I'm on Faery that I don't sense her presence. It was true even before I ended up with the land link."

"Tell me what to look for," I said. We'd comb the cave for clues. If we didn't find anything, we'd delve deeper.

"Anything that doesn't feel right," Cyn replied.

He returned to the side he'd begun examining. I took the other. Rather than eyes and ears, I used my psychic senses. As soon as they were fully dialed in, I felt the wrongness. "Something happened here," I murmured as I caught snatches of fury and disbelief. A struggle had spilled across the cave, one punctuated by betrayal.

Cyn was by my side in a heartbeat, magic looped in with mine as he sought to identify whatever had alerted me. I edged nearer the place that felt off. A declination in the crystals formed an alcove; I jammed my body inside and was nearly deafened by outraged howls that reverberated through my head.

Damn. It was Faery all right, but she needed words, not caterwauling. Cyn edged me aside, taking up the same spot I'd stood. It was a tighter fit for him, and his shoulders brushed up against the walls. I focused all my attention on the place our power slotted together, but try as I might, the yowling didn't turn into anything I could work with.

Cyn splayed his hands on the crystals. Blood flowed until it coated a few of them, and he began a low chant. I recognized the incantation. It was used to drag information out of unwilling participants. Except they were living creatures, where the crystals were collections of minerals. Cynwrigg held the land link, though. It might make all the difference. Presumably, the crystals and everything about

Faery were part of him. His blood should up the odds of us discovering what went on here.

I shut my eyes, willing whatever formed behind his third eye to play across my mind as well. Oberon and the Unseelie King came into focus, but grainy like an old black-and-white movie. They waltzed into Faery's cave and greeted her warmly. If they'd meant to set her at ease, it hadn't worked.

"What do you want?" she'd demanded.

"Is that any way to greet old friends?" Oberon simpered.

"The old part is correct. The friends part is not," she'd told him. "You promised to leave, yet here you are."

He turned his ringed fingers palms up. "What can I say, my dear? I couldn't stay away."

Meanwhile, the Unseelie king was edging nearer to Faery. By the time she noticed, he was almost within grabbing distance. She edged backward into the same declination where I'd stood. Gathering her dignity, she said, "Leave. You are not welcome here."

The Unseelie king spewed laughter, and I marveled that anything so beautiful on the surface could be so rotten beneath it.

"You will cede the land link," the Unseelie king told her.

"Nay. That will never happen." Faery stared him down.

Why in the hell didn't she leave? She could sink into the land, lose herself in its gullies and nooks and crannies. Instead, she glared defiantly at her visitors. A muted growl was the only warning before Medusa strode into the cave, snakes writhing, hissing, and spitting venom.

"We meet again," she announced cheerily.

Faery didn't reply. I sensed her working to extricate herself from the cave, but she should have executed that maneuver before the Gorgon made an appearance.

"Nice try, but you're not going anywhere," Medusa went on. "We need your help."

"I don't work for you," Faery growled, attempting to regain the upper hand, but it was hopeless against so many.

"You didn't before, but you do now," Oberon said not sounding nearly as cheerful. "After we've taken you down a peg or two, you won't be quite as capable of clinging to that land link."

The imagery winked out, replaced by blackness. "That's it," I said. "No other explanation. She's the power behind what they've done to resurrect the castle. They've trapped her somewhere, and they're draining her."

Cyn gripped the crystals tighter; his blood dribbled onto the floor. I shut up. He didn't need me Monday-morning-quarterbacking. When he finally let go and edged back toward me, he said, "I believe I know where they're holding her, but we can't go alone."

I sent jets of magic to seek out and destroy his blood where it was smeared on crystals and had dripped onto the floor. Blood holds power, which is why it's never wise to allow anyone free samples.

"Thanks," he said. "I'd have done that before we left."

"Where is she?" I asked. "All I saw was darkness."

"I recognized the feel of the place," he told me. "An old fortification is located to the northeast, maybe a kilometer from Dubrova. Its foundations run deep. The enclave was our stronghold before Oberon decided he required something grander and built the castle."

"Why couldn't you sense where she was without us going through all this?" I spread my arms wide.

"The draw of the old fort was the rocks lining its foundations. Their combination of limestone and gypsum and granite produces a serious dampening effect. The abandoned buildings used to be a great place to hide out when I didn't want to be found."

Breath rattled from me. "Interesting. So, they drain the land, and it weakens your link. Even if the bond holds, it will hinder our efforts during the next battle."

Cyn grunted. "Yeah. Fuckers. They're cheating."

"Not if we rescue Faery," I said. "How many more of us will we need?"

"Lots. In fact, let's rustle up everyone who's ready. We'll attack them en masse."

A quick transport spell spit us out in the glade. The dragons had returned. Excellent. Nothing like dragon magic to even up sketchy odds. Cyn whistled shrilly, and projected his voice with magic. If the Unseelie had spies, they'd get an earful, but it couldn't be helped. Plus, I was fairly certain they hadn't infiltrated our camp again. Their last few forays hadn't gone well.

"Change of plans," Cyn announced. "They've captured Faery and are holding her at the old fort."

Ash lumbered to Cyn. "Are you certain?"

"Almost. I asked the crystals, and they spoke to me through the land link."

Ysir raced forward, his features twisted into a worried expression. "But the old fort was impregnable."

"Not today, it won't be." Cyn drew his lips back from his teeth in a snarl. "Oberon's not the only one who knows Faery's secrets. The outer wall has weak spots, but we'll attack from the air. Once we're inside, we'll throw the gates open for everyone to enter."

"Or leave, if the Unseelie are their usual cowardly selves." Ysir nodded briskly.

Mother joined me; her forehead was etched into resolute lines. "Did you see this in your glass?" I demanded. There was no right answer. If she had and kept her mouth shut, I'd be pissed. If she hadn't, what good was all that time she spent peering into the future?

"I did, but I wasn't certain until the dragon seers corroborated it. I was just on my way to locate you and Cyn when you returned." She grimaced. "Oberon is living on borrowed time."

"Oh really? Then how does he manage to slither out from under our grip every single fucking time?"

"Language," she admonished.

"Like that's important," I shot back with staunch instructions to focus, goddammit. I'd had plenty of opportunities to end Oberon myself and had stepped aside. By that token, I was as guilty as everyone else. "Have you seen Danu?"

"Not yet."

"We're leaving," Ash trumpeted followed by a set of coordinates.

Cyn's magic collided with mine, and we were gone in a cloud of sparks and enchantment along with Mother and Ysir. Titania shimmered into a partially corporeal form next to Ysir. "I was busy," she protested.

"This is more important," he told her. "Faery's been captured."

More of the queen took shape until she was mostly whole. "Serves her right for letting Oberon go," she said.

"I'm certain she doesn't require you to tell her that." Mother's words held a dry note.

"Quiet," Cyn admonished. "We're meeting the dragons at the edge of the nightingales' pool deep in the woods."

If our straits hadn't been so dire, I'd have chuckled. Nightingales and ancient trees were the stuff of fairytales. As trees came into view I half expected an Ent to come strolling forward. Tolkien had Fae blood, quite a bit, actually. Neither was he dead, but living out a cushy afterlife in the *Dreaming* surrounded by fans and foes, alike.

Some of us had been horrified when he'd drawn back the curtain for a peek at magic's inner workings. Others had cheered him on. It had been around the time Faery had been open for tours, so his revelations weren't as egregious as they might have been.

But what did I know? All that happened during my outcast days. The long years Faery was closed to me, and I was doing my damnedest to pass as a mortal.

"Dariyah?" Cyn nudged me. Something about his tone suggested it wasn't the first time he'd called my name.

"Front and center," I said.

He pointed at Ash and the other dragons. Mother, Ysir, and Titania were already mounted. I got the picture and clambered aboard. We were the forward guard. We'd attack from above. Once we were inside, we'd open the gates for the rest of our army.

CHAPTER THIRTEEN, CYN

How in the unholy fuck had Faery allowed herself to be captured? What was wrong with her? The Faery I knew would never permit such an event to happen. But it had. Rather than mulling over a mystery I couldn't solve, I searched the area, alert for threats. A world where Faery could be seized was one requiring absolute vigilance. Nightingales lived in the ancient trees; this was their breeding ground, but none were singing today.

I hadn't visited the part of Faery where the fort was in over a hundred years. Created from grit and dust and magic, it was old beyond remembering. Heavy on earth and water, air held the mix together. In that regard Faery was quite different from the dragons' home world. Fire Mountain was mostly fire with air to fan the inferno. Earth powers ran a poor third, and water was scarcely in the equation at all.

Dariyah and I rode Ash as we'd done before. The dragon stretched his golden wings and soared upward, flying just above the canopy of trees. He must have hatched a plan with the other dragons because they spread out like spokes on a wheel. When the ones farthest from us turned, I figured they'd reached the gates surrounding the fort.

I'd shrouded my power, not wanting to draw undue attention our way until we were visible. My efforts to conceal us were pointless, though, because enchantment poured from the dragons. Anyone magical would have noticed them from kilometers away. Columns of Faery's warriors approached in four lines, each angling for one of the gates. When this structure had been built, the buildings ran along a north-south axis with gates situated at the four major compass points.

Ash waited until all dozen dragons were in position, and then they furled their wings, borrowed heavily from magic to keep themselves airborne, and held their circular formation until the ground rose up to meet us. The large courtyard appeared deserted.

It made sense with all the Unseelie we'd seen ranged around Dubrova. Once we'd taken care of the clones, their numbers weren't limitless.

Power pulsed from Dariyah in small, discrete bursts. "Not finding much of anything here," she murmured.

"They're underground," I told her, certain I had to be right. The crystals wouldn't have lied about something so basic as the whereabouts of their mistress. Sending a jet of power at the nearest gate, I sprang the latch bar and instructed the other entrances to open as well. Faery's troops marched through.

After jumping down, I waited for Dariyah and said, "Time to join your company." I'd have preferred to have her next to me, but I wouldn't belittle her skills by suggesting she couldn't take care of herself.

"I'm not familiar with this place."

"It's all right. Ulane will know which way to go, and your group won't be first."

With a terse nod, she ran across the courtyard to a group of warriors. Ysir, Auril, and Titania did the same. I angled my head upward and told Ash, *"We travel the midnight paths."*

"The ones that end up in Hell?"

"The same. They are narrow and winding. You may not fit."

"That's my problem to solve." Ash gestured at the other dragons; they formed a circle, power flickering around them as they worked out how to jam their bulk into corridors never meant for anything larger than a unicorn. More likely, they'd teleport to the bottom and hope the halls facing Arawn's realm hadn't fallen in. Several large chambers had been excavated hundreds of feet below ground, not because they fronted on Hell—that had been accidental—but because they offered a place Faery's mages could escape notice.

Our early days had been far bloodier. I remembered taking refuge in the caves more than once.

The fort hadn't changed much that I could see, which

offered hope the rooms beneath were still intact. My original home was constructed of rough-hewn timbers, flat rocks, and magic. One long wing was bisected by a much smaller one in the middle that had once held kitchens, a smithy, and a well-stocked alchemy lab. Not much we couldn't cobble together in that lab. It was where I'd honed my magical talents.

Me and every other young mage. Somewhere along the way, we'd almost quit producing children. Part of the bane of being immortal is worlds fill up, so there's no need for more mages. We'd lost something, though. Youthful energy and enthusiasm would have provided a needed counterpoint for Oberon's dour bigotry.

I hurried to the group I'd led during our last battle, joining Ysir, and we moved into the fort. Titania's group was ahead of us, Dariyah's right behind with Auril bringing up the rear. I kept my magical hackles deployed, hunting for evidence the fort had been invaded. So far, we appeared to be alone, but the foundation stones hid a lot.

Once there'd been three routes to the bottom, but it was too many to keep an eye on. Anyone who breached the fort's defenses could create problems. Oberon had jettisoned two of the paths, leaving the largest intact. Broad enough to accommodate four abreast, it would enable us to move quickly. We passed through the great room. Empty of furnishings, tattered wall hangings remained, lending the place a sadly abandoned look.

The kitchens took up two levels, and we transited the trapdoor that led downward. Naturally, it stood open when

I got to it, but had it been disturbed? I wanted to ask Titania, but I'd do that later. Layers of earth would shield our approach in the same manner it was shielding Faery and her captors.

The smells of damp earth and small rodents filled my nostrils, familiar and reassuring. If Gorgons had passed this way, surely their stench would have lingered.

But if Gorgons weren't here, I'd been dead wrong about where they were holding Faery. Damn it. I should have done this alone, as a scouting mission. In my haste, I'd siphoned all Faery's protection away from both Dubrova and the Midnight Court. Had I unwittingly played right into someone's hand?

The tail end of Titania's soldiers halted. I leapfrogged up the line to see where she'd stopped. It was at a sealed off junction point to one of the tunnel systems we'd shuttered. Power flickered around her as she assessed the choice point.

"Not a good place to stop." I pitched my voice for her ears only.

She rose on tiptoe and placed her mouth next to my ear. "Something is off. The farther down we go, the worse it feels."

I'd been checking, but hadn't felt anything. "Show me," I said.

She took my hand, sharing her magic. Everything changed around me. How could I have been so blind to evil creeping along the same corridor and stalking us? At least I hadn't been mistaken about Gorgons being here. And a

Harpy too. Their wings must have grown back in. Riding a hunch, I punched through the earthen wall separating us from the shuttered pathway.

Fresh, clean air wafted through the hole, so I did a quick and dirty job hollowing out a doorway. 'Much better," Titania murmured, "so long as we don't run into a major cave-in that blocks the way."

She ran through, her troops strung out behind her. I fell in at the head of my own group. After a section littered with rockfall, the path cleared. Why hadn't I felt the rot until Titania touched me? Was someone manipulating the land link to lure me? Surely, they'd figure I'd discover Faery's absence and come after her, but they shouldn't be able to touch the land link. I hadn't been able to all those years Oberon clung to it after he'd left Faery.

And I'd tried several times. It would have been by far the simplest way to deal with his stubborn refusal to let it go.

We plunged downward. Had not teleporting to the bottom been an error? I wasn't certain quite what we'd find down there. If the chambers had fallen it, extricating this many would take time we didn't have. The more I kicked the problem around, the surer I was I should have come alone.

Dariyah would have wanted to join me, but two is far more manageable than hundreds. Too late now. I'd set wheels in motion. We'd have to see them through to wherever they led.

We charged along the deserted tunnel. The farther we

went, the more confident I was it would take us all the way to the bottom. I'd forgotten how far it was, or maybe being centuries younger had made a difference. I kept testing the channel for the same darkness I'd sensed above. Not that I was the best bellwether, but Titania would stop again if she sensed evil closing its hooks around us.

Landmarks flashed by, gouges in rock I'd left long ago to mark my progress. A couple more switchbacks and we'd be at the bottom. Another sealed doorway should mark the far end. Sure enough, the column came to a halt. I joined Titania in front of the final barrier to what had once been safe haven.

Her hands were splayed across the earthen wall as she hunted for clues.

"Doesn't matter what you find," I told her. *"We're going through."*

"Timing is everything," she said, not bothering to take her attention from the wall.

I joined my power to hers, feeling the thrum of Faery through its queen. I might hold the land link, but Titania was bonded to this realm out of a lifetime of love and duty. The distinctive bite of dragon power blasted me. Without exchanging a word, Titania and I raised magic and blew the sealed gateway to bits. Dirt and rock spewed outward. The moment an opening formed, the same sense of impending wickedness pummeled me. And the place I was linked to Faery jolted into action. Finally. Thank all the gods I hadn't guessed wrong. For most of our downward trek, I'd been second-guessing myself. And then third-and-fourth-guessing.

Titania turned to the satyr standing behind her. "Magic at the ready," she instructed. "Send it up the line."

I stood aside while she and her warriors bolted through the breach. My group went next. We were in the largest of the four excavations. Mages flowed around me as Faery's warriors fanned out, forming an assault line.

Faery's physical form was lashed to the far wall with iron chains, but I was almost certain she'd abandoned her body. She'd made do without it for years, and something about the set of her head slumped on her chest suggested she wasn't much more than a sack of skin and bones, albeit a bloody one. Someone had opened her flesh with a whip. The rents should have healed immediately. That they weren't lent credence to my theory.

The Unseelie king turned toward me and smiled. A long, nasty-looking whip was clutched in one hand. Barbs hung off strips of leather. "Well met, Cynwrigg. I was expecting you, but not everyone else." He smirked. "Makes me feel important."

"Don't flatter yourself," I gritted and addressed my next words to Faery's assembled warriors. "Hold your positions," I said. "Wait for my command to engage."

Dariyah glided to my side. "You again," she snarled at the Unseelie.

"So nice to be recognized," he purred.

Meanwhile a surreptitious combination of magic and my eyes suggested the only other foe we faced was

Medusa, but her sisters could materialize at the drop of a hat.

I started toward Faery with Dariyah pacing me. The king stepped in front of us. "I cannot allow you to free her, Cynwrigg."

"You're going to have to stop me," I told him and feinted left.

Medusa spread wings that had, indeed, healed and blocked my way in a second direction. My nostrils recoiled from the acrid stench of poison as her snakes' tongues darted this way and that, shooting toxins all around me.

"Granny." Dariyah offered a brilliant smile. "Couldn't stay away, could you?"

"You are not my blood," the Gorgon said stiffly. "I just checked. Your claim was a misbegotten trick to force bad blood between my son and the Unseelie, a stunt you unfortunately accomplished. And one I will never forgive you for."

"Guess again." Auril pushed away from the troops that spread behind her. "Danu did a bit of rearranging. She found your son's blood...repulsive."

"Shut your damned mouth," Medusa shrieked. "I should have killed you on my island."

"You tried and failed," Auril reminded her in the same saccharine tones.

Time to step in. We were getting off point. "You're going to lose," I told Medusa and the Unseelie king. "You're outnumbered. Badly."

"Are we now?" Medusa batted long lashes my way. "So

long as we keep Faery captive, we hold a lot of your power along with her."

"We're here, dearie," Aello trilled as she, Ocypete, and Celaeno surged from shadows.

This was getting better by the moment. I knew I'd smelled Harpy. "Guess we'll find out," I told Medusa. After building a ward around Dariyah and me, we started toward Faery again. Freeing her body would be a gesture, nothing more. She wasn't in this room, but she was close.

I'd definitely felt dragons. Where were they? I trusted Ash, but he could show up anytime. My goal was to extricate Faery's warriors without casualties, and it was looking as if we might manage it. We'd need them all to take on the Unseelie squatting next to Dubrova.

"Enough!" a deep voice boomed.

Certain it had to be trickery, I kept my gaze glued on Medusa, the Harpies, and the king. Their expressions suggested if there were deceptions in play, they weren't of their making.

Oberon chose that moment to glide between two boulders and lay both hands on Faery's abraded body. The word "enough" hadn't come from him. I'd heard his whiny voice often enough to recognize it in my sleep. "Let me save you," Oberon crooned to Faery.

His pretty act didn't last but a few seconds before he spun and faced the winter king. "What have you done with her?" he shouted.

"She's right there." The King of Winter cast a glance at Oberon that suggested his associate had gone mad.

"The body, aye, but the rest of her is gone. Fool!" Oberon screeched. "You've been played, and you didn't even know it."

"Careful." Medusa's gaze shifted from me to Oberon to the Unseelie king. "Who knows which side Oberon is on these days."

"His own," I said acidly.

"Some things never change," Titania tossed out.

"And I said enough." A tall gaunt man swathed in a black robe emerged from nowhere. Black hair swirled around him, and his dark eyes shot darts of pure outrage. A large golden ring set with black onyx graced an index finger, and his feet were encased in tattered sandals.

Auril hurried forward and bowed her head. "Uncle. It's been far too long."

"Move aside." He swept past her. "Next time you choose to visit, call ahead."

Realization hit me in the guts with all the subtlety of a roundhouse punch. This had to be Arawn, Celtic god of the dead. I'd met him a time or two, but so long ago, I'd forgotten what he looked like. We were within spitting distance of his realm. All the shouting had no doubt disturbed him. I'd always heard he kept a firm rein on his charges and his domain.

Dragons poured into the cavern from one side. The other Gorgons leapt through a gash in the ether with a couple of men I didn't recognize. Probably Infernals tagging along for a bit of fun.

Jagged lightning exploded from Arawn's raised hands.

With laser-like precision, bolts pinned Gorgons, Harpies, and Infernals to a wall. "Anyone else feel like causing problems?" Arawn arched dark brows.

No one moved. The god of the dead planted himself in front of Oberon. "We had a bargain."

To my surprise, Oberon bowed low. "Aye, we did. Coming to this spot was not my idea."

"I do not care whose idea it was. You are here. In direct violation of a blood oath. Your life is forfeit. You shall do my bidding for the rest of forever."

"Please, sire. I held the compact sacred for many years. Give me one more chance," Oberon whined.

I watched with interest—and satisfaction. Apparently, we hadn't abandoned the fort for the reasons I'd thought. Arawn had wearied of having us so close to his precious dead and forced Oberon's hand, a niggling fact he'd failed to mention at the time.

While cleaving Oberon's head from his body would have given me a great deal of gratification, Arawn's solution was better.

"If you decide you don't want him, I'll ensure he never bothers anyone again," I offered to be on the safe side.

"Silence, or you shall join him." Arawn didn't so much as spare me a glance. He thumped both hands on Oberon's head. I expected piteous yowling and more pleading, but for once Oberon maintained the composure befitting a king. His body took on a glowing quality before it flowed to nothingness.

Dropping his hands to his sides, Arawn backed up until

he faced everyone. "Ash. You should visit more often—and under better circumstances."

"Agreed, and you are always welcome on Fire Mountain." The dragon focused his whirling gaze at the god.

"As are you and your dragons in my realm." Arawn paused. His gaze settled on me, reminding me of every incident in my life where I'd somehow fallen short. Immortal or not, someday a reckoning would come.

"The rest of you are not wanted here." Arawn's deep voice echoed off the rocks. "Finish whatever has been started, but you cannot do it here."

A tide of strong enchantment rolled through the cavern. Power pummeled me, burning, aching, stinging. Skin being flayed from my body would have been easier to endure. Breathing was tough, worse than the overheated air of Fire Mountain. I expected the spell to drop me somewhere, but when it cleared, I stood in the same spot with Dariyah next to me. Everyone else was gone.

"Where are they?" I asked. Addressing Arawn so abruptly was rude, but I had to know where my people had gone.

"The location this battle should have been conducted in the first place."

Dariyah fanned her wings outward. "Why are we still here? Our place is with our troops."

Faery's body jerked, and the chains holding it to the wall fell away. She walked forward slowly. "I am why you are still here."

"Her essence was safe in my keeping," Arawn said somberly.

I bowed my head. "Thank you."

Arawn placed a hand on my shoulder. "Look at me." When I did, he went on, "Faery is overdue for a change of venue. The outcome of the war will determine many things. Danu came to me—and others—requesting we assist. Except we steer clear of affairs not directly our own."

"Is Danu still helping?" Dariyah asked.

"I do not know. Many of us tried to disabuse her of her misplaced kindness, but her daughter and granddaughter are caught in the crossfire. Gwydion, fool that he is, lives for conflict. What would you expect from a master enchanter turned warrior? No one else was tempted."

At least it answered who might sign on as allies. I turned my attention on Faery. She looked worse than I'd seen her, but then I wasn't used to her corporeal form, either. "Are you ready to leave?" I asked.

The wounds crisscrossing her body had begun to heal. I took it as a good sign. "I am, but before we go I must tell you...things."

I shook my head. "No need. You are fully committed to our cause now. It's all that matters." As soon as the words were out, I knew how fervently I meant them. I didn't need deathbed confessions or promises to be better. What she'd done—or hadn't—would remain her secret.

Faery squared her shoulders. "Why are you being kind? I don't deserve kindness."

"We all do," Dariyah told her firmly.

"But I treated you horribly."

Dariyah shrugged. "All is forgiven. Let's go kick some Unseelie ass."

Arawn winced. Hidden away from the world, he'd probably had zero exposure to how gritty language had become. "Set your spell to bring you out near the castle—or what's left of it."

"Would you mind if we returned later, when all this is over?" Dariyah asked.

His brow developed furrows. "Why would you want to?"

"Mother called you uncle. It means you're kin to me. For most of the years of my life, Mother was the only blood relative I knew about. I'm intrigued by the rest of the family—those of you I never knew existed."

The stern cast to his face softened. "Aye, when you put it that way, you'd be most welcome."

"And me?" I asked in an attempt to clarify whom the welcome mat was meant for ahead of time.

"So long as it's only the two of you," Arawn said. "And now I must return to my duties. The dead do not do well if left alone for long."

After he'd faded from view, Faery tucked a spell around all of us. "Our first stop is the crystal cave," she said. "From there, we will determine the optimal place to"—she glanced at Dariyah—"how did you put it? Kick some Unseelie ass."

Dariyah smiled, warm and genuine. "Let's do this. I want Faery whole again."

"It might look different than you envision," Faery murmured.

Dariyah may not have heard her, but I did. Rather than chewing over what she meant by her statement, I readied myself to fight. The place the land link was anchored within me thrummed brighter than it ever had. More than anything, it told me Faery had been forthright when she said she'd finally chosen whom she was willing to fight for.

CHAPTER FOURTEEN, DARIYAH

Forgiveness is a funny thing. Once I decided to let my unsettled feelings about Faery slide, they departed without fanfare. One minute I was still steeped in petty—and not so petty—grievances, the next I was free. I'd made my share of bad decisions, so it would be disingenuous of me to hold hers against her. I was grateful Cyn had cut her off before she launched into true confessions time. For one thing, we needed to join the battle. For another, I really didn't care what she had to say. Nothing could justify some of her actions, and the future was far more important than the past.

I hadn't necessarily agreed with stopping in Faery's cavern, but the crystals took on a pale-blue glow, almost as if they were greeting their mistress. Had they sensed she was in trouble? It seemed likely since everything in this land was connected.

"Both of you, take hold of a crystal," Faery instructed.

"Why?" Cyn asked.

I expected her to huff outrage at being questioned. Instead, she said, "It is the final step in the bonding ritual for the land link."

Small lines radiated outward from the corners of Cyn's eyes suggesting he was beyond pissed she'd failed to mention he needed to do something to cement their partnership. He gripped crystals, one in each fist.

"Why me?" I asked.

"Because you are his mate."

I didn't question her further, just took hold of two crystals. They vibrated gently, growing warm beneath my touch, as calm rushed through me like an incoming tide. I wasn't sure what I'd expected, but this wasn't it. After the rough scrape of Arawn's magic, I'd expected pricks and pokes and sandpaper rubbing. The whole thing was over in less time than it takes to tell about it.

"We can go now," Faery said.

I glanced her way, blinked, and looked again. She was the same, yet not. Or maybe she hadn't changed at all. Perhaps I was seeing her through different eyes now that she'd added us to Faery's mysteries. I'd sort everything out later—assuming we had a later.

The Harpies and Gorgons and whoever those dudes down below had been would be shoring up the King of Winter's troops.

"Where will we emerge?" Cyn asked.

"Beneath the castle, and we're walking, not using magic

to get there." She pushed on a particular set of crystals, and a section of wall swept inward.

Cool. A hidden door, complete with a spiral staircase winding upward. I started up them after Faery with Cyn behind me. The thump of the door shutting behind us might have been ominous were it not for the mini-binding ceremony that established a connection between me and the land.

Faery including me said she'd let the bad blood between us go. We wouldn't ever be BFFs, but we could work together because I finally trusted her. I'd assumed we'd have to cover some distance between the cave and castle, but after climbing maybe fifty feet, another door opened into a place I recognized: Dubrova's lowest level. The one housing old dungeon cells and reeking of spilt wine.

The din of battle jangled discordantly even through the castle's thick foundations. I picked out dragons trumpeting and the clash of blades. Faery turned to us and touched our shoulders. "Doesn't matter what Auril or the dragon seers foretold, this will be the final battle of this war," she said. "We must prevail."

"You'd mentioned you had to remain no matter who wins," Cyn said.

Faery raised her gaze to his. "I believed it to be true until Arawn offered me sanctuary. Much as he did when I fled to his realm to escape the torture my body had become. The only reason it worked was because he was so close."

She drew her brows together. "If things go badly for us,

the two of you must retreat to Earth—or somewhere. Take your time, let years pass so our enemies grow complacent. When the time is right, find me in the halls of the dead. We shall strike when the Unseelie least expect it and return Faery to those of us who love her."

It was strange hearing Faery refer to herself as something outside herself, but she was both the land and its ruling deity. "I thought you said this was the last battle," I sought clarification.

"For now, it is. My vow to you," Faery continued, "is to hold the land link dear. If things do not fall our way on today's field, no one will wrest it from me. Arawn and the other gods shall see to it."

"Good enough," Cyn said and turned to me. "We shall fight side by side. Our troops are functioning under their second-in-command leaders."

"Works for me," I told him. Most of the mages in my group knew more about warfare than me. I was fine with it. They'd taught me a lot.

"I will be many places," Faery said. "You will know where I am, though. Feel me within you."

I checked, and son of a gun if she wasn't there alongside the places I shared power with Cyn and the dragons and Danu. Sheesh. Mother hadn't been kidding about the goddess marking me. She'd carved a trench a mile wide. I'd take it though, and all the magic I could lay my hands on.

"Assume a position on one of the turrets," Faery suggested. "Mages will see you and be heartened by it."

"What turrets?" Cyn asked. "They're rubble on the

ground."

"The castle should be nearly whole," Faery explained. "That Unseelie bastard dredged a lot of power out of me until I escaped to the halls of the dead." She cut a gash in the dank, wine-saturated air and stepped through.

Cyn's magic surrounded me. "I'm taking us to the top floor. From there, we'll climb to one of the parapets."

I'd been ready to get this show cooking since before we left the caverns under the old fort. Leaning into Cyn, I inhaled his whiskey-and-wildflower scent and readied defensive magic. It jumped to my call so fast I smiled ferociously. Something had shifted in the crystalline cave. The role Mother envisioned for me had finally come to fruition. I was Faery's protector, along with Cyn and the dragons and all of her courageous mages.

I didn't know quite what to expect. Faery had said the castle was whole, and the rubble piles I'd imagined never materialized. We came out in an upstairs hallway that probably looked the same as it always had. No shards of broken glass, no globs of mortar. The carpet was a little on the dusty side, but perhaps it always had been.

Had every stone found its rightful place? Had the window panes snapped back together? In a structure built with magic, anything was possible. Cyn took off for the end of the hall. I followed closely as he opened an unmarked section of wall that led to a short flight of stairs on our way to the roof. Hidden doors were starting to be a theme, except this one didn't clank shut behind us like the one guarding the passageway out of Faery's cave.

Whatever had been driving her when she kept a toehold in both camps? Had she been hanging onto hope Oberon would come to his senses? They'd ruled Faery for long enough their relationship had probably developed much like a bad marriage with enough feeble bright spots to offer false hope things weren't as crappy as she'd thought.

The encapsulation of Faery as an abused wife was funny in a black humor sort of way. My mind was all over the place; I reined it in. The rumble of battle grew in intensity until I plastered magic over my ears to tone it down. Cyn grabbed hold of a short ladder that spit him out on a catwalk between two turrets. I leapt lightly to his side.

Together, we surveyed the field far below. Columns of our soldiers clashed with Unseelie. Shouts, victorious and pain-laced, smote me. Above us, dragons shot fire at Harpies and Gorgons. Vipers jumped gaps in an attempt to poison the dragons, but they'd taken smart pills after one of theirs had fallen to such shenanigans.

From what I could see, each viper was immolated with fire nearly as soon as their mistresses tossed them at a target. "We need to fight," I told Cyn and spread my wings. "Standing around up here like a fucking figurehead isn't my style."

Ash thudded down, wrapping his rear talons around a parapet wall and keeping his wings extended for balance. "Get on," he said.

I longed for the freedom to fight my own battles. Amazing how quickly I'd grown used to the wings I'd looked askance at. Cyn clambered up until he sat astride the dragon's broad back. Maybe because I'd hesitated, he said, "Go on. Do your thing."

"Really?" The exhilaration from bloodlust snatched me up.

"Be careful," Ash growled. "You'd be safer on my back."

"I don't want safe." The words escaped despite my efforts to hang onto them. "I want to fight for Faery." She was part of me now, even with our rocky beginning. I wove lethal magic into a net suspended between my hands and launched from the parapet. I felt the backwash from Ash's wings as the dragon took off above me.

A Harpy closed from one side. Not Aello, but one of her sisters. Her teeth were bared in a snarl as she jockeyed to get close enough to hypnotize me. Whether she could was up for grabs. With all the veins of power running through me, I might be immune to her soul-stealing, but I wasn't willing to test the theory.

I waited until she was near enough to believe she had me before I banked until I was nearly above her and dropped my net. It snagged on her wings, and she couldn't cut through it. Shrieking imprecations at me, she plummeted from the sky.

I felt like dusting my hands together, delighted my ploy had been so successful. No time to rest on my laurels, though. I settled for a loud *whoop* and fashioned a second net. Because I'd already built one, I was quicker this time. When Aello winged toward me, hellbent on retribution, I led her on an aerial chase. My wings were bigger than hers. It meant I could fly faster, but she was more maneuverable. I watched carefully to learn the moves she favored. Part of defeating an enemy is being able to predict what they'll do next.

This Harpy wasn't as dumb as the first one had been. Or maybe she was doing the same thing I was: checking my moves. In an unexpected somersault, I ended up directly above her and dropped my net. It wouldn't kill her, but she'd be out of the game for a while, along with her sister.

"Nicely played," a dragon trumpeted as he (she?) flew past.

I built another net, larger this time. I wasn't expecting the last Harpy to get anywhere near me, but the Gorgons were doing an epic job reconstructing wings burned by dragon fire. If I could get a net around their wings, it would hold the fire in place so it could do more damage.

Maybe they'd tapped into my strategy because Medusa and one of the other Gorgons approached from opposite sides intent on trapping me. I only had one net, but even if I fashioned another on the spot, I couldn't be in two places at once. While I was tossing a net over one Gorgon, the other would nab me. I could almost see it playing out, and I'd be damned if I'd end up fodder for their mill.

I couldn't outrun them flying, neither was I more agile than they were. While I'd developed a comfort zone in the air, they'd been flying for thousands of years longer than me. I raced through possibilities and only came up with one that didn't require a dragon-assist.

I hate asking for help. It's like cheating. Besides, I've always prided myself on working alone. Yeah right. Misplaced pride if there ever was such a thing because what choice had I had before this? Including mortals in my squabbles was forbidden, and I'd steered clear of the rest of the magical world to preserve my Witch illusion. Glamours fell apart if anyone examined them closely. It was why I'd been so surprised Oberon took my presentation at face value and didn't bother checking its accuracy.

Meanwhile, the Gorgons were dipping and weaving like scissor blades. A viper fell onto my shoulder. I swept it off before it could dip its fangs into me. But I was lucky I'd seen it. The snake had been tiny and well-shielded with its owner's magic.

I had to even the playing field, but could I get close enough to net one of these horrors? The dragons had noticed my predicament. Two flew between me and Medusa. It cleared the decks for me to do a back flip and toss my net over the other Gorgon. So much for my "I work better alone" theory.

The Gorgon, Stheno, turned end over end as she fell unable to escape either my net or the dragon fire that followed her to the ground.

"You little bitch," Medusa squealed. Vipers rained down on me. Crap. Had she emptied her head of them? I plucked three off, but one landed between my wings, and I couldn't reach it easily. I sent magic to stifle it, but I was too late. The bite of fangs sent bitter cold into my shoulders. It froze everything it came into contact with, and suddenly flight took all my concentration.

A red dragon flew beneath me, and I landed heavily on his (her?) back moaning in pain. There had to be a way out of this mess. I redirected magic as fast as I could now that I didn't have to worry about remaining airborne. While I managed to keep the poison from spreading farther, the upper half of my back felt as if it had turned to ice. I began to shiver, teeth chattering.

Ash and Cyn bombarded Medusa with fire and magic, not letting up until she fell from the skies. I was having a tough time hanging onto the dragon. My vision hazed over, and I couldn't feel my fingers or toes. Maybe I hadn't stopped the viper's toxin after all.

I felt Cyn's magic before he landed behind me. "Get her to the healers," he told the dragon.

"I should take her to Fire Mountain," the dragon rumbled around fiery belches.

"No time. I've called her mother and aunt."

Cyn's words sounded as if he were talking from the bottom of an echo chamber. My grip on consciousness was slipping away. I tried to tell him I loved him, but I couldn't get the words out. The ground rose up to meet us, and Cyn was running with me in his arms, dipping between lines of battling soldiers. He should be with his mages, not wasting time with me.

The landscape turned surreal, changing color from blue to purple to black. I lay on something. Not the ground, but close to it. Mother and Titania argued about something, their voices fading in and out. "For the love of the goddess, move, both of you," another voice thundered. Danu. I'd recognize her stentorian tone anywhere, even in my depleted state.

I tried to tell her I wasn't that bad. That I'd taken measures to stem the toxin, and it should play itself out. Eventually. She'd healed me once before, but then she'd anesthetized me. Either she'd decided I was tough enough to withstand searing agony, or there was no time for anything but an intervention. I'd only thought I was barely conscious. Pain ripped through me, bright, blinding, all sharp edges and pointed stakes. Screams tore from my throat. One after the other. Embarrassment swamped me, but I couldn't stop the caterwauling. Christ. What a ninny. I've never seen myself as weak before, but I was yowling like a scalded cat.

"Get hold of yourself." Danu stopped torturing me long enough to shake a long-nailed index finger in front of my fractured vision.

I swallowed the next scream. Choked on it, and did the same with the next, and the next. Somewhere along the way, the pain eased a little. Not much, but it didn't take much to be an improvement.

My eyes snapped open. I was panting and lay in a pool of sour-smelling sweat laced with the stench of viper poison. Had I sweated out the bad stuff? Whatever Danu was doing had settled down to a dull ache. I struggled to sit but didn't get far before I fell backward. "Got to get back to the fighting," I slurred.

"In a minute." Danu knelt and ran her hands over and under me and dragged me to a sit.

I cast my bleary gaze at my surroundings. We were in a clearing in the forest, and I lay on a field blanket. Danu and I were alone. "Where is everyone?" I asked.

"Fighting. Drink this." She thrust a flask into my hands.

My stomach recoiled at the smell. Rotten leaves, sulfur, and something decidedly alcoholic. Not wanting to look even more puny than I'd been, I slugged it down, gagging. Once I knew it would stay down, I pushed to my feet and smiled crookedly at Danu.

"Thanks, Granny. Looks like you're destined to be my guardian angel."

Her mouth twitched as if she were fighting smiling back. "The others could have saved you, but my way was quicker. Get back out there. We're not done yet."

"Are we winning?"

She drew her brows together. "Maybe. It could still go either way. I have work to do. You're far from the only casualty."

Before I could thank her, she was gone. Maybe it was her healing, or perhaps the horrible-tasting drink kicked in, but I felt like myself again. Not 100 percent, but not far from it. Raising my mind voice, I called Cyn's name intent on joining him.

"Dariyah?" His voice echoed through my head.

"I'm fine. I'll join you momentarily."

My message must have startled him because he strode

through a break in the air and wrapped his arms around me. "Are you sure you're recovered."

"Yeah. No mollycoddling. Let's win this bitch. I didn't like Faery's suggestion about lying low for a hundred years and revisiting it."

"Me, either." He kissed my forehead and let go of me. "We're working on the western flank. It's a ground war now. The Harpies and Gorgons are out of the picture. Our current targets are Shadow Lords and a couple of stray Infernals who are fighting because it's what they do. They'll lend their magic to any battle if it keeps them out there slugging."

"If we get rid of them, will the Unseelie go away?" I asked.

"If we get rid of them, I'm hoping the Unseelie will rejoin Faery," Cyn told me.

I opened my mouth to protest they were a pack of fuckers who didn't deserve to be here, but shut it damned quick. It wasn't my call, and Cyn had a point. A defeated enemy offered an olive branch can turn into a loyal ally.

Or they can stew in their own resentment and rise against you.

"Sure you're up for this?" Cyn was eyeing me closely.

"Absolutely."

He didn't ask again. I embraced the sweep of his power as it transported us to the western flank. As soon as his spell cleared, a row of Shadow Lords came into view. My throat was still raw from Danu's healing, but I loosed a bloodcurdling screech and hurled power at our enemies.

❧ 15 ❧

CHAPTER FIFTEEN, CYN

An hour earlier

Danu had chased us all out of the grove she'd chosen to work on Dariyah. I'd wanted to remain, but she'd made it clear she wouldn't lift a finger to save her grandchild if we didn't hustle out of there. It was probably an empty threat, but I didn't want to test it given Dariyah's precarious state. Besides, I had unfinished business with the Gorgons. They were dead meat. Not a one would walk out of here no matter how much dragon fire and magic we had to throw at the problem.

As a last resort, the dragons could haul them to Fire Mountain and cast them into fiery pits where they could burn and regenerate and burn again. Forever. I rather liked the idea.

"It will be right," Auril murmured next to my ear. "Mother likes her."

I bit my tongue before the obvious question popped out, which was what would happen if Danu didn't like someone who was gravely injured. It was moot because the goddess wouldn't have jumped into the middle of this if she hadn't had good intentions. She'd been having too good a time fighting alongside Gwydion. Warrior magician and master of illusions, he'd heeded her summons to combat.

I'd never met him before; neither had I had a chance to get close enough to thank him for his aid since he was on the ground and I was in the air. With ice-blond hair braided close to his head, a burly build, sea-blue eyes, and a magical glowing staff, he looked imposing, and dangerous.

When I realized Dariyah was in trouble, I'd left Ash to deal with the flying monsters and teleported onto the dragon carrying my mate to safety. I owed that red beast a lot. He'd stabilized Dariyah with magic, so she didn't fall from his back before I arrived.

After a nudge from Auril, and another from Titania, we left Danu to her healing. She was wise to force us to leave. Dariyah's screams rang through our link, and it took all my self-discipline not to scurry back and throw my body over hers. Yeah, and if I'd done that, I'd probably have sabotaged her chances of recovering. The Gorgons' vipers carried poison augmented with magic. It had nearly been the death of Auril on Medusa's island.

As I neared the field, I considered how to proceed. I could jump back onto Ash, or I could fight from the ground. A hasty magical scan told me all the Harpies and two of the Gorgons were down here. It decided things. I warded myself so I wouldn't get sidetracked by my own troops needing something or enemies out for my head. Everyone would be better off if I eliminated the possibility of viper poison or soul-snatching. Forever.

The dragons had created a ring of fire around Stheno, Euryvale, and the Harpies. What the hell had happened to Medusa? The Gorgons and Harpies were trying to regrow their wings to escape the fire, but the dragons were doing a bang-up job keeping any new wing feathers smoldering. Before, the Harpies' wings had been unaffected by flames. The dragons must have found a magical work-around.

I couldn't penetrate the fire circle from my side any more than those within could escape. It cast my next moves in a different shade of revenge. I rejoined Ash to buy myself a vantage point to launch lethal magic. "They need to die. Permanently."

"They will. We have a plan in motion. Dariyah is recovering?"

"Yes. Danu is tending to her."

"She couldn't have better care," Ash rumbled.

I started to ask about Ash's plan when Gwydion loped into view. A cross between an ancient Viking warrior and a vengeful god, he split the fire circle with a fountain of water. The flames closed behind him, and he swatted Ocypete with the butt end of his staff. Carved of something impervious to flames, it glowed an angry red as he pounded her skull to a pulp.

"Regent," he hollered.

I teleported to his side. "What do you need?"

"Focus destruction here." He jammed the bloody end of his staff at the Harpy's destroyed neck. "Keep it going until I tell you."

Faery wove the land link into my magic. I felt the alteration when she joined me. The Harpy's human half cleaved in two, the sections falling to both sides as they turned black and rotten.

"That should do it." Gwydion sounded positively delighted. "Now do the same thing for this one."

I moved to Caleano. This time, death came quicker because Faery was already riding shotgun. I didn't require Gwydion's instructions to approach Aello. She promised me riches, eternal youth, a free ride out of every dicey situation, and a cavalcade of virgins to fuck. I killed her before the last of her inducements were done.

I was getting on board with Gwydion's hearty delight in slaying our enemies. The one I wanted, though, was Medusa. She'd harmed my mate. "Who's next?" I asked the master enchanter as he brandished his bloody staff.

"Who do you want?"

"Medusa, but she's not here."

"The dragons took her," Euryvale squawked.

This was getting better and better. I turned to her and pulled my blade of infinite shapes. "You'll do in her place." I grinned as savagery raked me, and I swung my blade, severing head from body.

It wouldn't kill her, not without an assist, but getting those fucking snakes out of the way was a strong start. I kicked the head with my booted foot; it flew through the air and was immolated in dragon fire from above.

Damn it felt good to have companions I could count on. I'd been stuck with Oberon so long, I'd forgotten what loyalty and commitment felt like.

Gwydion raked his staff down the Gorgon's headless body, separating her ribcage as he went. Snakes crawled from the body cavity, but they were tiny and frightened as they scurried for cover. I'd had no idea the Gorgons created their own vipers.

"She won't bother anyone again." Gwydion spit on her remains before we converged on Stheno. She raised eyes that no longer spun to me and Gwydion. "Please. I am the last. I give you my word, I'll trouble you no more, nor anyone else, either."

Gwydion moved closer, staff raised.

"Hold," I said and strode between them. My blade took its usual, much smaller form, and I made a cut in the ball of my thumb. "Blood bond," I told the one remaining Gorgon. "You will retreat to Sarpedon Island and never leave."

The Gorgon tore a hole in her hand with her teeth and offered her streaming palm. "Blood bond," she agreed. I set a magical barrier so her blood couldn't enter my body and touched my cut to hers.

"That was stupid," Gwydion snarled.

I turned to him. "Maybe so. I might live to regret freeing her, but I will ask the dragons to escort her home since she cannot fly. While they are on the island, they will erect barriers she cannot cross."

"It's fine," the Gorgon croaked. "So long as I get to go home, nothing else matters."

"You say that today," I admonished her, "but your relief will shade to anger and resentment. If you plot against me and mine, I shall finish what Gwydion and I and the dragons began. Do we understand one another?"

"We do." She bowed her head. With her slumped shoulders and burned wings, she didn't look like much of a threat, but I wasn't fooled.

The dragons had been listening. A blue one swept low, grabbing her in his rear talons. I turned to Gwydion and held out a hand. "I appreciate you being here."

He clasped my hand. "You're joking, right? I live for battles, and they're few and far between these days. Our next stop should be to the west. Shadow Lords and Infernals are raising hell. If we rid ourselves of them, everyone else will go home."

Dariyah's voice in my head was welcome. I thanked Gwydion again and teleported to where she was, mostly to reassure myself she was as recovered as she sounded. And to make certain she wasn't alone in the battle that still raged. I soft-soaped that part. She wouldn't take being watched over well.

I brought us out on the western edge of the field across

from Shadow Lords and the men I'd seen below the old fort.

Dariyah delivered a ferocious cry, and launched herself into the fray. Bones littered the ground where Gwydion, Ysir, Titania, and Auril had dismantled some of the Shadow Lords. They were already dead, and it appeared they went the way of Vampires, turning to bones and dust once whatever animated them was interrupted.

Dragon fire didn't have much of an effect. No part of the Shadow Lords burned, not even their robes. How in the hell they managed that was a mystery, and not one I was likely to solve. I liked them better when they degenerated into heaps of moldy bones.

Blade in hand, I tag-teamed fighting one of them with Dariyah. Hovering a meter or so above the ground, she drove her boots into his face. The crack of bones was satisfying, but they began to knit back together immediately. Ysir thrust a vial of dark liquid into my hand. "Toss it into his mouth. Should do the trick."

"What is it?"

"A little of this, and a little of that. Ask me later."

I moved close, sword at the ready, and waited until Dariyah kicked in the ghoul's teeth. When he was bouncing backward from the strength of her blow, I leapt up and poured the noxious stuff into his gaping mouth.

He gagged and tried to spit it out, but the angle was wrong. I suspected even if he'd been able to double over and spit, Ysir's concoction would still have worked. The

Shadow Lord developed a translucence and collapsed, twitching, as his body disintegrated to nothing but bones.

Dariyah landed next to me and fist pumped the air. "What was that shit?"

"No idea. Ysir's private stock of poisons."

Gwydion sidled near. "Three to go." He sounded disappointed the fun was nearly over.

"They're yours if you'd like," I said.

"Bull crap. I want at least one more," Dariyah cried.

"How about if we do the last three together, niece?" He smiled warmly.

"I'd like that."

Gwydion draped a muscled arm over her shoulders, avoiding her wings handily, and the two of them ducked to avoid a volley of black darts aimed right at them.

Between the dragons and Gwydion, Dariyah was in safe hands, so I landed back on Ash. "Could we have a fly over?"

The dragon nodded. "Everything is winding down, but a whole lot of Unseelie are still standing."

"Do you know where the King of Winter is?"

"I do." Ash flew toward the knoll behind Dubrova.

I had good intentions, but I wasn't a fool, so I tested the waters with telepathy aimed at the Unseelie king. *"Will you parley?"*

"Cynwrigg?"

"Who else?" I wasn't in the mood for games.

"Aye. I would parley. Where?" A terse note suggested the

Unseelie thought I was up to no good. I didn't blame him. In his position, I'd assume the same.

"Dubrova's courtyard by the castle doors."

Ash landed, and I waited still astride him in case the Unseelie showed up with a band of warriors intent on playing dirty. Trust was in short supply between us, but we'd have years to mend that problem.

So long as he saw the wisdom in my offer.

Minutes dripped past, so many I was getting ready to leave, when the King of Winter walked around the castle toward me and the dragon. A quick look-about with magic proved he'd come alone.

I jumped down and waited for him to draw near enough to talk.

"I have a proposal," I told him.

"I'm listening."

"We have lost many good men and women and animals during this wholly unnecessary fight. I propose a truce, and I offer you and yours safe return to Faery to live among us once again."

His silver-gray eyes widened. Clearly, it wasn't what he'd expected me to say. Probably he'd anticipated something more along the lines of his head rolling at dusk—and then a truce.

"It's more than generous," he said. "Certainly not in line with Oberon's policies."

"I am not him. Thank all the gods for small favors. He is gone forever. Something that should have happened the moment he decided Fae were better than every other iteration of mage."

"Will you be Faery's ruler?"

"I will. And I aim to be both just and fair. If you accept my offer, I hope you and other Unseelie will be part of our new court system. Different from the structure Oberon established, it will be inclusive and take the voice of all Faery's citizens into account."

The King of Winter smiled and walked forward, hand extended. "I accept on behalf of my people. Some may wish to remain on other worlds, but it's good to have choices."

"I won't apologize for destroying the place you'd been living," I told him. "It was a grim compromise, and we were at war."

"I understand. I'd have done the same. That world was harsh, but it was all we had. And why Oberon's offer to join forces was so compelling."

Dariyah and Gwydion ran up to us. "It is done," she said. "No more Shadow Lords. No more Infernals."

"And no more Gorgons or Harpies." Gwydion dusted his big hands together after balancing his staff against a thigh. "A good day's work all in all."

Dariyah looked from the Unseelie king to me. "Offered him amnesty, did you?"

I nodded. "Aye, and he has accepted."

Dariyah stalked forward until she stood toe to toe with the King of Winter. "You made Mother's life hell. She gave up a lot to get away from you. If you come back here to live, you will leave her in peace."

"I promise," he said solemnly. "You no doubt view me as insufferably chauvinistic, but you are young as mages go. I wasn't much different from other men. It's not an excuse, merely an observation. I've learned a lot. I loved your mother, and I drove her away from me."

"We'll have time to hash everything to death later," I told him. "Call off your army. I shall do the same. We will have a feast tonight at the Midnight Court. I hope you'll join us."

"Is that an open invitation?" Gwydion asked after the Unseelie walked away.

"Of course," I told him.

Faery stepped through a gash in the air. "That was the right thing to do," she said to me. "Oberon lacked compassion, and it was the death of his kingship. Rulers with no heart turn sour, and everything they touch withers and dies."

"Was that what was happening to you?" Dariyah asked and reached for Faery's hand.

The land deity clasped it and nodded. "It was slow, but I was rotting from within. I didn't have any choice linked to Oberon."

Ash trumpeted and puffed steam over all of us.

Faery extended her other hand to me so the three of us were joined. "Tonight at the Midnight Court, you shall be crowned king and queen of Faery. I decree it."

"Cyn already knew," Dariyah said. "He saw it in a dream or a vision."

"More of a putting two and two together," I said and bowed my head before the land. "I will do my best to do right by you, but if I slide off the rails, tell me right away when there's a chance to correct whatever isn't working before it becomes entrenched."

"It goes both ways," Faery said solemnly.

All around us, distant cheers erupted as the message the war was over moved from group to group. I didn't have to tell Faery's warriors after all. The King of Winter was doing it for me.

"I will return this evening," Ash said, "with a full contingent of dragons. But you must come to Fire Mountain too, so we can celebrate properly as befits those carrying dragon magic."

"We will," I assured him before he departed in a flood of sparks and dragon enchantment.

"Let's walk the field," Faery said. "I want everyone to see us together and be heartened."

Hand in hand, the three of us started for the gates circling the courtyard intent on doing right by those standing and the fallen on both sides. The Unseelie would receive heroes' funerals too.

"How are those plans coming along for the court of destiny?" Dariyah asked.

"They're coming," I said.

"Good name." Faery smiled. It lightened the austere cast to her features.

"And apt," I said. "We rose to the challenge and made our own destiny."

"It wasn't looking very promising," Dariyah said.

"Maybe not, but I never stopped believing in Faery's potential."

"I didn't make it especially easy," Faery murmured.

"Ssht. No looking back," I told her.

We reached the first group of soldiers and stopped to share their relief and joy they could lay down their arms. Life could get back to normal, not tomorrow but eventually. After cries of, "See you later at the Midnight Court," we moved on.

✤ 16 ✤

CHAPTER SIXTEEN, DARIYAH

Mother and Titania and Danu and I worked over the wounded for hours. While we served the living, Cyn and Ysir and the Unseelie king sent the dead to the afterlife with several unicorns helping out. By the time we ran out of mages to heal, hours had passed. Night had fallen, and it was time to convene the Midnight Court. I hoped someone had made food because I was starving.

It would have been nice to clean up, but I had nothing to wear here. Not much point in washing off the blood and dirt and remnants of my sour sick-sweat if I got back into the same old stinky clothes.

Mother beckoned, "Come with me."

"But you have to open the court."

"I just did. Come with me," she repeated.

I followed her to her cottage. A group of nymphs met

us at the door. Chattering animatedly, they led me to a copper tub filled with scented steaming water. The lure of being clean overshone not having anything fresh to wear, and I stripped off my filthy field clothes. The trousers had so many holes, I'd probably chuck them.

Mother bustled out of the cottage, and I sank into the tub inhaling rosemary, lemon, and a mix of other herbs. The nymphs wanted to wash me, but I drew the line at handmaidens, so they offered me soaps and traded buckets of dirty water for clean ones as the water became grungy.

I could have stayed in that tub until it turned stone-cold, but Cyn was waiting for me at the Midnight Court. He'd made choices today, carved a foundation for the kind of king he'd be. One who was firm but compassionate. One who didn't hold grudges. I was proud of him and eager to stand by his side. Not to claim any of the glory, but to support him in what was bound to be a challenging and difficult transition. Distrust for Oberon was deeply ingrained. Cyn would have to go above and beyond to win back the love of his people.

I still didn't see myself as Faery's queen. That role rightfully belonged to Titania. While I felt sure I'd carve out a place for myself in Faery, I wasn't certain yet exactly what it would entail. I'd been a child of the streets, keeping to the edges of mainstream activity. Clinging to a low profile wouldn't work here.

Eh. I'd figure it out. I always did.

After dragging my hair through the water one last time and picking a few remaining bits of bone out of it, I pushed to my feet and took a robe from one of the nymphs, wrapping it around myself. Another handed me a towel, and I used it to soak water out of my hair.

"Is there a hairbrush or a comb?" I asked the nearest nymph, a tiny faery with violet wings.

She gestured me to a stool. Above my protests, she and two others proceeded to work the tangles out of my hair. Every time I tried to wrest an implement from them, they flew out of reach. I hadn't realized how tense I'd been, but between the bath and the nymphs fussing with my hair, something that had been tightly wound inside me began to relax. As the faeries worked, they funneled magic-laden warm air to dry my curls, and they fluffed around my face and shoulders.

I still couldn't quite believe I wouldn't get up tomorrow and prepare to fight some more. I'd been fighting all my life. Or hiding. Change would be more than welcome. I'd embrace it, and I'd fashion a spot for myself here. No reason to rush anything.

"Oh good, you're out of the bath." Mother's voice preceded her as she swept into her cozy home with clothing draped over an arm. "Here you go. Put these on."

She'd cleaned up too and changed into the richly embroidered robe I'd seen before when she presided over the Midnight Court. "You should have said something," I murmured. "I'd have taken a much shorter bath, and we could have shared the tub."

"Nonsense." She waved me to silence. "You'll move into

Dubrova soon. It's little enough time I'll have you close by."

I hadn't exactly thought about where I'd live, but I'd assumed Cyn and I would split our time between Earth and Faery. I didn't want to give up my home on Earth—or my kitty—although having an escape from the summer heat would be welcome.

I stood over a long dark skirt painted with runes and glyphs in silver. Running my fingers over its exquisite workmanship, I reveled in its fine weave before sliding it over my hips and stepping into a pair of sandals not unlike the ones Mother favored. A matching tunic had cutouts to accommodate my wings, and I slid into it.

"Wow. A perfect fit. Wherever did you find these?" I asked Mother.

"I didn't find them, I had them made for you," she replied.

Turning to look at her, I asked, "When?"

She smiled. "Never could get much past you. I had these made before we left Faery."

"Before I was even born?"

She nodded. "I knew you'd have wings. I just wasn't certain how they'd manifest. I guessed at how tall you'd be, but those garments are a decent fit."

A chuckle rippled from me. "Eh, maybe there's more to all that seer mumbo-jumbo than I gave it credit for."

She laughed. "There might be. Hard to say." Walking behind me, she clipped something heavy and cold around my neck. It warmed quickly, and I examined it with my fingers.

"Gold?"

"And a moonstone," she said. "It's a gift from Danu, and now it's time to join the festivities. You too," she told the nymphs who'd been emptying the tub with thimble-sized buckets. "Don't worry about that, I'll take care of it later."

With a flurry of wings, they flitted through the door with me calling, "Thank you," after them.

Mother hooked a hand around my arm. "You look every inch the queen you are."

We walked from her cottage toward the glade, and I said, "But Titania is the rightful queen of Faery."

"She was, but her time has come to a close. Even she realizes it and is more than a little relieved to become Faery's dowager queen." Mother lowered her voice. "All of us recognized how damaged Oberon was, but she was closer to him than the rest of us. She gave up trying to change him, which meant she sat by while he presided over atrocities. Trust me when I say she's been ready to step down for a long while."

"Did she know I was slated to take her place?"

Mother stopped walking and turned to me. "Nay, dear. Not even I knew, not for certain." She kissed both my cheeks. "We've traveled a long road, you and I. Not so long ago, I didn't believe I'd see you again, but destiny intervened."

"There's that word again," I murmured.

"Aye, 'tis alive and well in your soul. I knew you'd shape

your own fate. You were stubborn and strong-willed even as a child. I rarely interceded because you'd need every bit of that strength and more to fulfill the role I'd thrown you into when I followed my conscience and lay with Pegasus."

We began moving again. The altar where Mother presided over the Midnight Court came into view. The glade overflowed with mages and animals. Cyn turned toward us and extended both hands. It was tough to keep walking. What I wanted to do was stop and stare at him. His fair hair had been washed and brushed till it shone. Tiny jewels were woven into its strands.

White leather trousers encased his long legs; matching lace-up boots hit him just below knee-level. A tunic embroidered with depictions of every mage and animal in Faery swathed his torso. His arms were bare, and a bronze torc circled his neck.

Mother stepped off to one side, and I walked into Cynwrigg's arms amid cheers, whoops, and shouts. Faery's mages wished us a long and happy life together. Animals large and small surrounded us, chittering and purring and woofing. Hawks and owls and ravens flew circles overhead, landing occasionally. The blare of dragons trumpeting drew my eyes upward in time to see the skies fill with dragons of every color, all puffing steam to wish us joy.

"The land is whole again," Cyn said. "I feel the differ- ence in my link to it. It's joyful, no longer divided against itself." Letting go of me, he turned to face his people with me by his side. Dragons skidded in for landings all across the green.

Not far from us, Pan and several satyrs were tuning up their instruments. Danu, Gwydion, Arawn, and others I didn't recognize—but presumably more deities—stood near Pan and his musicians. Everyone was so resplendent, it was tough to believe we'd been wallowing in blood and dirt only a few hours before. Speaking of which, I picked Unseelie out of the crowd. It made my heart glad so many had taken Cyn up on his offer to rejoin Faery. Their world had been such a shithole, I felt almost sorry for them.

Faery's unique magical energy vibrated through my bond with her, so she had to be close. Sure enough when I scanned the crowd, I spotted her regal form gliding toward us. Garbed in another fancy robe, this one pale violet, she carried an old-fashioned lantern in one hand. Its amber glow lit the path in front of her, and people moved aside, bowing in deference to their land-liege.

She stopped in front of us and raised the lantern until we were bathed in its glow. "I will keep this short," she said. Although she was turned away from the assemblage, her throaty voice carried. "Faery, the new Faery, will be a home for all magical beings. Everyone will have equal standing and a voice if they wish to help govern our land."

Faery took a breath before addressing Cyn and me. "Do each of you promise to rule my land with the best within you?"

Cyn bowed somberly. "I do, my lady."

"As do I," I said, adding, "Titania, please step forward."

My aunt made her way to my side, a creamy silk gown

billowing about her and her white hair done up in an elaborate chignon. "Aye, dear, what is it?"

"Are you certain you don't want to continue as queen of Faery? By rights, it's your..." I faltered. Job wasn't quite right. Neither was role.

Titania saved me from floundering about searching for a term that fit. "Quite certain, niece. Now, if you'd like to sign me up as advisor, I'd be delighted, but I'm more than ready to pass the torch." After giving me a kiss on the cheek, she walked over and joined Mother.

"Anyone else you need to question?" Understated humor ran beneath Faery's query.

I shook my head. "Nope. Nary a one."

"Then we shall proceed," she said. "You, Cynwrigg ap Llyr and you, Oonagh Morgan ferch Llyr, shall rule Faery. You shall speak for me, act in my stead, and rule with justice and grace..."

I'd stopped listening, and what I did next was probably inexcusable, but I blurted, "That's my name. My true name." It wasn't a question. Once I heard my name it resonated within me, pinging sweetly off my magic.

Faery stopped talking and focused her burnished metal eyes on me. "Aye, child. First you've heard it?"

"It is." I swallowed hard. "Why ferch Llyr, daughter of Llyr, when Pegasus was my father?"

Danu loped toward me. "I fixed that problem," she informed me. "You may claim Llyr as a distant father since his blood flows through nearly everyone here."

Fascinating. So she really had obliterated the winged

horse. It would have been nice if she'd asked me, but all I'd have wanted was to ensure I hung onto my wings, and they hadn't gone anywhere.

Faery chopped a hand downward. I shut up. Plenty of time to sort my proper name and parentage once she was done. "As I was saying," Faery continued. "You shall rule on all matters, and your word be deemed law."

Raising her arms above her head, she turned to the crowd. "Welcome your new king and queen."

The roar that thundered through the group nearly deafened me. Cyn threaded an arm around my waist, and we faced the assemblage. Faeries and nymphs fluttered near, pelting us with flower petals. For the first time in forever, I stopped worrying about the future and sank into the moment.

Faery had revealed my name. After longing to know what it was since realizing Dariyah was a placeholder, I was shocked how little difference knowing made.

Cyn placed his mouth near my ear. "You've always known who you are. What difference does a label make?"

I turned in his arms and kissed him. When I lifted my mouth from his, I replied, "None at all."

Pan and the satyrs began to play while we stood and shook hands with everyone who wanted to wish us a wise and prosperous reign. Somewhere along the way, food and drink materialized, and I remembered how hungry I was. Finally, our impromptu receiving line ran out of people. Faery was long gone. Wise of her.

All around us, mages chatted and sang and ate and

made love. Cyn took my hand, and we joined in the revelry. We'd earned this respite. Tomorrow, we'd begin shaping the Court of Destiny with participation from as many of Faery's citizens as wanted a say in their government.

But that was tomorrow. Tonight, I'd kick up my heels, dance my heart out, and make love. Cyn whooped, I hollered, and we joined the nearest line of dancers.

You've reached the end of *Court of Destiny* and the series Magick and Misfits. There may be a fifth book. You never know how these things shake out. But for now, I'm moving on to my next series, Circle of Assassins. Please leave a review for *Court of Destiny*. Do it now while the story is fresh in your mind. Doesn't have to be fancy, a line or two will do it.

If you missed my Gatekeeper series, read on for a sample from *Shadow Reaper*. If you enjoyed Charley Daniels, you'll love Kate Carrick, the reaper assigned to Vampire duty.

BOOK DESCRIPTION, SHADOW REAPER

The dead are restless, and a whole lot less cooperative than they have been. That was true even before I drew the short straw and ended up with Vampire duty.

Since then, Reaping has taken way more time. So much, I'm worried I'll lose all the clients from the career that actually feeds me. I run a small private pilot school. It pays most of the bills and means I don't have to keep regular hours.

Death wants me to remain in one piece. She's bailed me out often enough, she's all but ordered me to find other employment. I just smile and nod after our little talks, and then I climb back into a cockpit.

Our last toe-to-toe didn't go so well. She went and assigned Vampires to me. That's when Reaping turned into a million-hour-a-week job. I can almost hear the Reaper who was stuck with them before, laughing his head off.

I shepherd souls to the other side. Vampires have zero interest in leaving, but I have a quota to fill. Means I have to trick them, but it didn't work for long. They're onto me. Damn Death, anyway. She painted a target on my back, and now the Vamps are out for blood.

In more ways than one.

SHADOW REAPER, CHAPTER ONE, CAIT

The screen on my crappy monitor looked blurrier than usual, but it might have been my vision. No sleep these past few nights had to be taking a toll. I rubbed grit out of my eyes and shut them, promising myself it would only be for a couple of seconds. Then I had to get back to last month's books.

They weren't looking good. I'd spent more on mechanic bills and aviation fuel than I'd made. Big surprise. To teach flying, I have to actually be here. Not off chasing Vampires. A sigh started in my chest and burbled out my mouth before I could stop it. Sighing is for wimps.

I'm more of a take-charge type. Or maybe I'm deluding myself.

A pair of ghosts drifted through the far wall, making a beeline right for me. They were on the youngish side, maybe late forties when their lives had been cut out from under them. I'm a Reaper, and souls who have yet to cross are drawn to me like the proverbial moth to a flame. It's a scent thing, kind of like pheromones, except keyed to crossing the veil rather than for sex.

They say hearing is the last sense to go. Nope. It's smell.

I stood and flapped my hands at the approaching pair. "Find another Reaper. I've been reassigned."

"But we're here," the man protested.

"Here," the woman echoed.

They were only a few feet away. A closer look revealed bullet holes in both their foreheads. Crap. Had they been victimized by another mass murderer?

"Please," the man said. "Winnie and me, we—"

"Nope." I turned both hands palms out. "Determining where you end up is above my pay grade. Sorry you're dead, but telling me how it happened is a waste of your time."

At this point, acting as a conduit was simpler than arguing. I covered the remaining distance between us and opened my arms. The duo didn't require further instructions. They walked into my embrace, first one then the other, more than ready to depart this portion of their existence. As I held them, they passed through me.

My Reaper side channeled the dark forever of death, and a chill I knew all too well shot from my toes to my head. If I'd had any hopes of finishing my bookwork, it just went up in smoke. Or ice chips. Reaping is hard work. There are several of us, but never enough to go around.

Fuck it.

I sat back down. Next I pushed the keyboard aside, folded my arms on my dusty desk, and laid my head on top of them. A fifteen-minute nap would do me wonders. Maybe after I finished the books, I'd clean my office. Customers offered pilots latitude when it came to neatness, but I'm not sure I'd climb into an airplane with someone whose workplace looked quite as down-at-the-heels as mine.

Carrick Sky Sports is located in a small Quonset hut right next to the hangar housing my three planes. The hangar was a whole lot cleaner than my digs, but then so were the planes.

I took care of them. They were my babies. Thoughts of airplanes and Vampires and Reaping whirled through my tired brain before I finally nodded off.

A staunch knock startled me so badly, I nearly tumbled out of my chair. It skidded back a few inches, leaving me fighting not to end up on my ass.

"Cait Carrick?" a deep male voice inquired.

I had yet to get a visual on the speaker. At least he wasn't dead. Their voices lacked resonance.

"Yeah. Um, yes. That would be me." I stuffed my feet under my body and stood, turning until I faced the single door into my office. I'm tall, so tall I'm used to looking down at everyone, including men, but the dude who stood there was at least six foot four, topping me by a good two inches.

Faded Levis encased his long legs. Torn trail runners might have been black once, but they'd faded to gray. A battered leather vest and frayed blue-plaid shirt covered his torso. Fair hair was long enough for him to have gathered it behind his head into a ragged braid. He had an interesting face, all planes and angles with a square chin and sharp cheekbones, but his most unusual feature was his eyes. I suppose they were hazel, but in the light streaming through the door behind him, they glowed like burnished copper.

"Sorry to disturb you." He grinned rakishly. "I tried knocking softer, but you were really out of it."

I swallowed back annoyance. I'd be damned if I'd stand here while a total stranger blithely assessed my physical state.

"And you are?" I raised my eyebrows.

"Liam. Liam Hunter." He glided toward me, hand extended.

Something about him bothered me, but I couldn't home in on what it was. I tucked my hands behind my back. "Sorry," I mumbled, "I've got grease all over me. What can I do for you?"

"They say you're the best flight instructor around." His smile, which had slipped a few notches, bloomed again.

"Who's they?" I winced. I should just have said "thank you" and let it be.

"Why all the pilots down at *The Tailwind*."

It was a small bar and grill at the far end of the airstrip I used. Most days, they served breakfast and lunch. Weekends, they served dinner. While I knew all the local pilots, I wasn't aware they ever talked up my skills. Most of them were pretty old-school. Chauvinistic enough to believe women belonged in the kitchen—or the bedroom—rather than in an airplane.

I'd dealt with a lot of flak a decade ago when I opened my business. Once the guys figured out I wasn't a flash in the pan, they dialed back the harassment but never totally accepted me.

What to do about the dude standing three feet away?

He had an expectant look on his face, as if he'd offered up the aeronautical equivalent of "Open Sesame." If I didn't have so many unpaid bills, I'd have chased him out of my office. On the other hand, I didn't want to share a cockpit with someone who started out on the wrong foot by lying to me.

I pushed my shoulders straighter. If I'd gotten any mileage out of my nap, it wasn't readily apparent. "Um, look, Mr. Hunter—if that's even your name—the other pilots would never steer business my way. Either you play this again from the top, or we have nothing to talk about."

His smile developed a definite sheepish cast. "That transparent, huh?"

I nodded and waited, too tired to spar with him. Night would fall soon enough, and then I'd be back to herding Vampires. Death wanted them in Hell, but they were a slimy, sleazy lot with a huge investment in remaining on Earth.

There it was. My problem in a nutshell. Their motivation in staying topside was significantly more pressing than my need to move them across the veil. I'd quit if I could, but Reapers are born into Reaping.

And we live for a very long time.

The thought of chasing down Vampires until the moon fell out of the sky depressed the living fuck out of me.

"Ms. Carrick?"

I started. I hadn't exactly forgotten Mr. False Name, but he'd moved away from dead-center on my radar. He kicked the door shut. A surge of magic flickered around him, turning the air as blurry as my monitor had been.

"You're right about me being tired," I told him. "If you're about to cut the crap and tell me who you are and why you're here, we'll both be money ahead."

The angles in his face grew more pronounced, his fingers more elongated, the copper cast to his eyes deeper, shinier.

I narrowed my eyes. "Sidhe or Fae. Am I right?"

"Aye, Ms. Carrick. I'm Daoine Sidhe. Liam is a modernization of my name, and my family name is Warwick." His accent had shifted from pure American to a lilting Irish brogue, or maybe it was Scottish. Never could tell them apart.

Breath hissed through my teeth. At least he'd offered his true name. The teensy jolt I'd gotten from the other one hadn't bothered me this time. "You scarcely need my airplanes. You can teleport."

The corners of his generous mouth twisted into a wry expression. "You know about us?"

No point dancing around what I was. I was certain he

knew, and my soul-herding skills were why he was here. "I went to Reaper school. We have to get passing grades before Death turns us loose."

He furled a blond brow. "Fascinating. I had no idea."

"How about if you tell me why you're here? Then you can leave. I have work to do." A quick glance through my single window told me time was about to betray me. Sunset would be in maybe an hour. With it would come the Vampire horde blood-bent on my destruction.

Or my assimilation, to be more precise.

He frowned. "You're about to have company. I shall return later."

Before I could tell him not to bother coming back, the place he'd stood was empty. I could still feel the beat of his soul, but damn if he hadn't vanished before my eyes.

I stared at the door. I might not know Mr. Warwick, but I trusted his paranormal ability. Sure enough, a knock was followed by a swoosh as the door flew open. Kiko Tanaka strode inside, dark hair billowing around her head like a cloud. She's my closest friend, and another pilot when she's not busy being a pharmacist. Her Japanese heritage is evident in her slight figure and dark, almond-shaped eyes.

"Not late, am I?" She grinned at me. It lightened her features and made her look about sixteen.

I must have appeared blank because she added, "Remember? You promised me an under-the-hood check ride."

Heat rose to my cheeks. "Sorry. I didn't exactly forget. But it's okay. I have time."

"Are you sure?" Kiko asked. "You're looking a little ragged around the edges."

"Yeah. I'm sure. I'm good for a check ride." To avoid more commentary about how trashed I appeared, I strode to the board and snapped up keys for the Cessna 172. Like I said, I have three airplanes, a Cessna 152 trainer, the 172, and a Piper Seneca. The Piper is a twin-engine jobbie. It costs me five hundred bucks an hour to keep it in the air, so I rarely fly the old girl. She's left over from when I used to have a contract for air freight runs. Then she made sense because she has a great payload.

I really should sell her, but I don't have the heart. Like I said, the planes are my babies.

We left the Quonset hut with Kiko chattering a mile a minute about a hunky dude she'd met the night before. I kicked back and let her manage the preflight checklist. She's efficient. No wasted motion. She even remembered to grab the cushion that made up for her short arms and legs.

She took the left seat; I settled into the right as she nosed the Cessna out of the hangar. I love the moment when a plane is barreling down a runway, gaining the momentum it needs for its wings to carry it skyward. Once we were upstairs, Kiko tugged a hood over her head and proceeded to follow my instructions using the instrument panel rather than her eyes.

We're both IFR certified, which means instrument

flight rules. It's the step that comes after VFR. All pilots have to be able to manage their planes under visual flight rules, or they don't get to fly anything.

Didn't take long before we were circling to land. Kiko did a great job, flared at just the right time, and the plane settled gently to the tarmac, right on the numbers at its eastern end.

"Do you want her back inside?" Kiko asked. Her hood lay across her lap. She'd removed it on our final approach.

I shook my head. "Think I'll take her back up for a bit."

She taxied the plane off the runway and patted my thigh. "If there's anything I can do, just holler."

"Thank you." What I didn't say was that talking about my particular problem wouldn't solve anything. She offered up her logbook, and I initialed our check ride.

"I'll leave a check on your desk," Kiko told me. Pushing the door open, she climbed down. I handed her pillow outside before I switched sides of the plane. She knows what I am, but not about my Vampire-herding assignment. I'm not about to tell her—or anyone else, either.

Magic came out of the closet about fifty years ago, but the presence of supernaturals makes most mortals really uncomfortable. If it had only been one variety, things might have gone smoother, but when it became apparent the dude next door could be a witch or a shifter or a Druid or one of the Fae, a backlash developed.

Humans still aren't certain Vampires are real. The fuckers are masters at hiding the corpses they've drained. And the newly turned ones are kept on a very short leash.

Over time, the friction between mortals and magic had done nothing but grow worse. Lots of anger and hatred on both sides of the fence. This group, Humans Rule, has been a particular thorn in my side. Mostly, I keep a low profile and stay out of everyone's way, though.

I have enough problems without turning into a crusader for magic wielders and our rights.

I nosed the Cessna back into the air, glorying in the feel of the plane as I put her through her paces. She's a good compromise. Light, reasonably fuel efficient—for an airplane—and responsive. The sky to the west lit with what was shaping up to be a glorious sunset. On a whim, I flew into it, chasing the colors across the Olympic Peninsula.

When I finally turned back to the east and set the three-axis autopilot to take me home, I considered how to spend the coming evening. Really only two choices. I could barricade myself into my houseboat on Lake Union.

A fortunate choice of residences since Vampires hate water.

Or I could go hunting. Problem was, I'm about out of tricks. Vampires are very old. Even older than me, for the most part. With age comes shrewdness. Because they all talk with each other in some perversion of telepathy, I can only use a strategy once. They were onto me. It was either come up with something new or lie low.

By the time my wheels kissed the tarmac, I'd come to a decision. I had to have another sit-down with Death. If she wanted to purge Earth of Vampires, maybe she had some ideas—other than driving the Reaper assigned to them nuts. The guy before me had done pretty much nothing. It's not like Death can fire us.

I considered my options as I taxied off the runway and into my hangar. I could follow the other Reaper's example, but it went against the grain. I'm not lazy. Beyond that, I do not like to lose. At anything.

Right now, I was slightly ahead. Majorly ahead, actually. I'd shunted an even dozen Vamps to their rightful spot, presumably in Hell. The way it works is this. I'm a gateway, a link between Earth and Death's domain. The dead pass through me, but I have no jurisdiction over their destination.

Better if I don't know.

I can't imagine a Vampire ending up in the good spot, though.

I buttoned up the plane and pulled the hangar door shut. It creaked on its rollers, and I added spraying them with silicone to my endless to-do list. Once the hangar was locked, I trotted to the Quonset hut. I was feeling better. Flying always lifted my spirits.

And I had a direction scoped out. My next heart-to-heart with Death had to happen soon. I'd make some notes, to be sure I didn't miss anything, and then I'd reach out to her.

It was full dark when I unlocked my office and walked through the door, clicking on the overheads as I passed the bank of switches. I returned the Cessna's keys to their hook on the board. Kiko's money was dead center on my desk. If I hadn't been so cash-strapped, I'd have told her the check ride was on the house, but av gas wasn't cheap. Last week it topped six bucks a gallon, and we'd burned through seventy dollars' worth before my solo indulgence flight.

My monitor had long since blacked out as my computer went into sleep mode. I considered returning to my book-work but didn't feel like it. The bad news would hold till tomorrow. Even without hard figures, I had choices to make. Either I freed up enough time to make *Carrick Sky Sports* profitable again, or I'd have to sell my planes. Hangar rent was two thousand dollars a month. Upkeep on the planes another thousand—if I was lucky.

Normally, it was doable. Flight lessons were expensive. And I could always bid to fly freight with the Piper Seneca again. But to do those things, I needed time. And a decent night's sleep every night. Not sleeping because I was on Vampire patrol was the linchpin that was killing me.

I rolled my eyes. What an unfortunate turn of phrase. I was only about six months into Vampire patrol, and I was sick of it.

Maybe thinking about the Undead drew them, but the lights flickered, and the chill of grave dirt descended on my head like a ton of bricks. Thank all the gods I had a moment's warning. It was enough for me to dash to the locker where I keep my street clothes and grab the saber I'd bought for just these occasions.

It had cost me an obscene amount of money, but the blade is a mix of silver and iron. Perfect for unruly Vamps and not quite as personal as impaling them through the heart with silver stakes. This way, the length of the blade is between us. Stakes would have required me to be right up next to the loathsome fuckers.

I swung the blade, ready for damn near anything. I'd taken a few lessons in swordsmanship once I bought the saber. Those were a bitch to find. It's not the Middle Ages anymore. Not too many knights errant wandering about running schools for wanna-be warriors.

My death-sense intensified. The smell of rot pervaded my office. Could they come in without an invitation? The lore suggested otherwise, but I'd run across the occasional Vampire in broad daylight, so the rulebook didn't seem to apply any longer.

Sure enough, one sashayed through a wall. I didn't bother looking at him. They're all hunks. And they all reek of decay. Another followed him. And another, until half a dozen formed a semicircle around me. I'd been savvy enough to place a wall behind me, or I'd have been surrounded.

Smart fuckers. They understood my blade would end them, so they kept just beyond its path. I glared. They glared back. Every time I made a move, they jumped nimbly out of my way. They're fast. Superhuman speed and strength comes along with the blood-spell that turns them.

Dawn might end my predicament, but I did not want to spend the next nine hours staring down the maw of a Vampire horde. More were joining the ones already here. Naturally. A telepathic summons must have gone out. My throat was dry, my breathing shallow. They'd planned this, probably just been waiting for a night when I was stupid enough to be in my office after the sun went down.

I raised my mind voice and shrieked, *"Death!"*

"She can't help you." A blond who could have been a cover model for GQ leered at me.

"You'll like us. Once you're one of us." A woman with long russet hair smiled, displaying her fangs.

Yeah. That is so not going to happen. I can't teleport, though. The floor wasn't about to open up and swallow me. If I charged forward, blade swinging, I might behead a few, but not before one of them sank his fangs into my neck.

I've been in bad spots before, but not quite this difficult. Better to go down fighting than cowering, though. With a pivot in what I hoped was an unexpected direction, I drove the point of my saber through a Vampire chest. It wasn't a silver stake, but it should work the same way.

The Vampire shuddered and collapsed. Where its body had been was a pile of moldering bones. I didn't even have to bother freeing my blade. The circle around me backed up a foot or so.

My breath came in ragged pants. I swung about and skewered another one. This Vamp was younger. Blood spurted from it, blackish ichor that outdid any charnel pit for stink.

Motion from the corner of my eye was the only warning I got. Swinging blind, I beheaded the Vamp trying to close on me from one side. Bones clattered as he hit the floor.

They could do this all night. I couldn't. I was already

woozy from six months of barely sleeping. Where was Death? She'd always come before when I called her. I'm a Reaper, not a soldier. Reaping is usually peaceful.

I silenced my mind. Feeling sorry for myself—or expecting help to materialize—were dead ends. At least it was late enough, no mortals were likely to show up. I didn't want to be the cause of anyone joining the ranks of the Undead.

Time passed. I stabbed, swung, stabbed some more. My head hurt. My hands hurt. My eyes were giving me trouble, refusing to focus. I can build wards, but not against the dead. It would be counterproductive since I'm supposed to be a beacon for them.

A burst of furious Old Gaelic battered my ears. Great. A Celtic Vampire. Just peachy. Had this bunch summoned the Undead version of someone like Sir Lancelot? I narrowed my eyes, but my vision was a joke. Blurry and caught up in the half-light common to the dead, I couldn't see a thing.

"Move over, Ms. Carrick," a familiar voice ordered just before a man slinging magic burst through a portal. I blinked against the glare arcing from his fingers.

"Liam?"

"Who in the bloody fuck did you expect? Santa Claus?" Intent on beheading Vamps with Sidhe magic, he didn't so much as glance my way.

I admit, I was slow on the uptake, but once it sank in I might not end up turned tonight, I waded into the fray, swinging my saber with renewed energy. Maybe Liam did something, but my lethargy dropped away. Once I had enough oomph to drag all of me back to the land of the living, my vision returned to normal.

My mind was firing on all cylinders again, and I didn't care for its conclusions. Liam wanted something. He must have wanted it pretty damned bad to show up now. Surely, his Sidhe magic told him what he was walking into.

I was grateful, sure I was, but also suspicious as hell. Why did I have the feeling death by Vampire might be preferable to the favor Liam was about to call in?

Tough to refuse someone who'd just saved my bacon. Tough, but not impossible. I cautioned myself to wait. Once we were out of this, I'd keep as open a mind as possible. At least listen to him before I said no.

ABOUT THE AUTHOR

Ann Gimpel is a USA Today bestselling author. A lifelong aficionado of the unusual, she began writing speculative fiction a few years ago. Since then her short fiction has appeared in many webzines and anthologies. Her longer books run the gamut from urban fantasy to paranormal romance. Once upon a time, she nurtured clients. Now she nurtures dark, gritty fantasy stories that push hard against reality. When she's not writing, she's in the backcountry getting down and dirty with her camera. She's published over 90 books to date, with several more planned for 2021 and beyond. A husband, grown children, grandchildren, and wolf hybrids round out her family.

Keep up with her at www.anngimpel.com or http://anngimpel.blogspot.com

If you enjoyed what you read, get in line for special offers and pre-release special reads. Sign up for my newsletter on my website or my blog.

Rhinna

Kylian

Coven Enforcers

Blood and Magic

Blood and Sorcery

Blood and Illusion

Demon Assassins

Witch's Bounty

Witch's Bane

Witches Rule

Dragon Heir (Summer and fall, 2019)

Dragon's Call

Dragon's Blood

Dragon's Heir

Dragon Lore

Highland Secrets

To Love a Highland Dragon

Dragon Maid

Dragon's Dare

Dragon Fury

Earth Reclaimed

Earth's Requiem

Earth's Blood

Earth's Hope

Elemental Witch

Timespell

Time's Curse

Time's Hostage

Gatekeeper

Shadow Reaper

Rebel Reaper

Untamed Reaper

GenTech Rebellion

Winning Glory

Honor Bound

Claiming Charity

Loving Hope

Keeping Faith

Ice Dragon

Feral Ice

Cursed Ice

Primal Ice

Magick and Misfits

Court of Rogues

Midnight Court

Court of the Fallen

Court of Destiny

Rubicon International

STANDALONE BOOKS

Branded, That Old Black Magic Romance (paranormal romance)

Edge of Night (short story collection, paranormal and horror)

Grit is a 4-Letter Word (nonfiction)

Heart's Flame (post-apocalyptic romance)

Icy Passage (science fiction romance)

Marked by Fortune (post-apocalyptic coming of age story)

Melis's Gambit (historical paranormal romance)

Midnight Magic (paranormal romance)

Red Dawn (post-apocalyptic paranormal romance)

Shadow Play (historical paranormal romance)

Shadows in Time (Highland time travel romance)

Since We Fell (contemporary romance)

Warin's War (paranormal romance)